Jules in His Eyes

Jules in His Eyes

Vivi Simone

ISBN-13: 9780692592014
ISBN-10: 0692592016

Dedication

This book is dedicated, first and foremost, to my boredom and to all of the time that would've been wasted if I'd paid attention in those unnecessary meetings that could've been summarized and sent in an email with the slide show presentation that was read to a room full of well-educated, well-trained, under-paid teachers.

To my husband Lewis, my best friend, my lover, my confidant, and my answerer of endless questions: Thank you for being my sounding board, my endless source of answers, and for always supporting me.

My stories are for my readers who just want to get lost for a little while.

Lastly, I dedicate this to the future because my children will go to college without financial aid or debt.

Acknowledgements

There is a team of people that made this project possible: Janet, Susan (Dauntless), Lindsay (Pirkleator), Abbey, and Julie—better support than an underwire bra. Without you ladies, none of this would be possible.

Also, thank you to all of the behind-the-scenes people that made this project possible.

My Stella Nova family: Jenny, Cheryl, Jesalyn, Nichole, Kelly, Kasey, April, Jennifer, Michelle, Erica, Courtney, Johnna, Malory, Noelle, and Melinda. Thank you for reading this before it was really going to be a book, and thank you for being interested in the project and listening to me talk about it for forever. Sherry, muchas gracias for fixing my Spanish. That was one of the funniest conversations of my life.

Heather—the Gayle to my Oprah—picture that white sandy beach and clear blue water that you know I'm not getting into with you. Find me on the beach, I'll have the green and the sun block.

Lastly, I acknowledge myself and urge her to stay on her grind to turn nothing to something.

Prologue

Four weeks before Jules Dempsey was to graduate summa cum laude from the University of Miami, Florida, also known as "The U," she was attending her grandfather's funeral with her aunt Leslie and Leslie's partner, Jackie, in Boston. She hated Boston and had been gone ten years; short visits were manageable, but the idea of spending any significant amount of time there sickened her, especially because there was someone there she definitely never wanted to see again. Instead of staying in Boston, Jules had chosen to attend college in Florida. She had taken a year and a half off after high school then spent the next seven years, intermittently, to double major in economics and finance. She also had minored in math and accounting.

Jules had plans to go straight to New York, where she had accepted a job offer as a finance manager from a woman for whom she had done some consulting work. Little did she know her dad had other plans, and her life was about to be put on hold then completely flipped upside down. She was already sad because her Poppy had died, but she was inconsolable when her father *told* her that the weekend after graduation she would be returning to Boston for the foreseeable future. They were all at her grandparents' house after the funeral. She was sitting in Poppy's recliner, pushing some food around her plate, when her dad sat down in the chair next to her.

"Jules," Thomas Dempsey said in a serious tone and thick New England accent, "when we come down for your graduation at the end of the month, you need to be packed and ready to go on Sunday."

She began to protest, but her dad held up his hand to silence her.

"I spent more than two hundred fifty thousand dollars for your education," Thomas continued, "and I don't have the money to put my mother in a nursing home. Assisted-living facilities cost a hundred grand a year, and those are the ones that are just a notch above shitholes. You're going to help your ma take care of Lovey. Your ma is so busy all the time. She can't just drop everything to take care of your grandmother."

Jules looked a little shocked as she asked, "How long is this supposed to last?"

"You'll do it every day until one day you don't anymore. Understand."

It wasn't a question. She nodded. Since Poppy was gone, Lovey was coming to live with her parents. Her grandparents' house was too big for her grandma to maintain or even clean, especially since she suffered from osteoarthritis, moderate glaucoma, fatigue, and diminished appetite. Even though moving in with Thomas and Helene was in her best interests, Lovey was as unhappy with the situation as Jules was. Although Jules and Lovey were tight, Lovey wanted to stay in her house, and Jules did *not* want to return to Boston.

Chapter 1

The plane was heading toward Logan Airport on a Sunday afternoon in May. Jules sat next to her mother and tried really hard not to be mad at her dad. About halfway through the flight—she figured they were somewhere over Maryland—her dad filled her in on the rest of the plans he had for her while she was "home."

"Your grandmother has physical therapy three times a week," he said. "Monday through Thursday she likes to go visit with friends. They play bridge or work out or play canasta. She also has monthly doctors' appointments. And while she's visiting and keeping her social calendar, you can come help me out at the office."

Jules closed her eyes and muttered, "Planning on getting your money's worth out of me, aren't you, Dad?"

He nodded. "Every penny, kid."

Jules's dad was a part-time attorney who kept an office in downtown Boston. He was also a representative of the Commonwealth of Massachusetts in the US Congress and had been a congressman for the last fifteen years. His constituents supported him and felt he was true to his word, which typically isn't a prominent characteristic among lawyers or politicians.

Jules wasn't even off the plane yet, and between her dad and her current location on the planet, her anxiety and nausea were at near-disastrous levels. She found herself praying to whatever life-force had created the earth and silently hoped the package her dad's sister, Leslie, had mailed would be waiting for her. The package contained several individually wrapped "graduation presents," with each present containing an ounce of weed; there would be a total of sixteen ounces altogether. As an added precaution, Aunt Leslie had lined the box with fabric softener sheets to mask any odor. On top of this, the entirety of Jules's life would be arriving soon by a truck, to be moved into the detached garage behind her parents' house. Somewhere, scattered throughout those boxes, were about six ounces of chartreuse-colored Jamaican bud that Jules had packed separately before heading to Boston.

As Jules's dad was gathering their luggage at baggage claim, her ma, Helene, turned to her and said, "A package came for you the day before we left for Miami."

"Who was it from? Do you remember?"

Her ma thought for a few seconds then said, "I think it was from Leslie and Jackie, probably graduation presents or stuff you might have forgotten to pack."

Jules managed a weak smile. She knew her ma was doing all she could to help her only daughter with this "transition." Jules really felt it was a step backward because she had decided ten years ago *never* to move back to Boston. This move wasn't her decision of course; it was a directive from her dad, and he did have a valid point. He had dropped a fuck ton of money on her education and never had said a word about it except "Finish." She had done that, with honors, and now her future had come skidding to a halt…at least for a little while.

The car ride home was a blur. From what Jules could tell, through barely open eyes, the neighborhood looked pretty much the same. Although people had made improvements to their houses over the years, and the landscaping varied from house to house, the neighborhood remained the upper-middle-class neighborhood she was raised in. Split-level, traditional two-story, and ranch-style houses lined the streets.

Jules's nerves were so wound up about returning that she was surprised she hadn't yacked in the backseat of her ma's BMW X3. A sadness had settled over her, as the knots in her throat and stomach tightened. This return was something she was going to have to get over, and she would, tomorrow. It wasn't exactly the returning—it was the staying that had her so freaked right now. *Deep breath in. Now exhale. Don't clench your jaws; it'll only make it worse.* Once they arrived at the house, she grabbed two of her bags and retreated upstairs, desperate to ease the nausea consuming her body.

The large two-story brick home looked the same as she remembered. When she was a child, the house, with its wide front porch and old wooden porch swing, was the only place she'd ever called home. Now she only thought of it as her parents' house. However, it looked like Helene had been making some home improvements. The front door and shutters, once burgundy, were now a light walnut color. Helene thought neutral colors brightened up her home.

Helene liked to redecorate periodically, so the interior of the house had changed some since the last time Jules had been home; that was three years ago when her ma had turned fifty. The foyer had a new walnut table, and the most-recent family pictures—from Helene's fiftieth, hung on the walls. A plush leather couch, the color of desert sand, sat in front of the TV, and a matching love seat sat in the corner. Her dad's well-worn La-Z-Boy was in its usual place, and the walls that led upstairs were still lined with pictures from the Dempsey children's childhood.

Her ma knocked on the bedroom door. "*Ma petite bijou,* are you hungry?"

Jules shook her head. "*Non, Maman,* not right now. I'm going to unpack some things and take a shower."

Born in Paris, Helene had moved to the United States with her parents when she was nine. All three of her children understood more French than they could speak. They all favored one another, as siblings tend to; Aaron and Chris especially shared a strong resemblance. They were a good mix of their parents, whereas Jules looked much more like Helene. The boys were both tall; Chris was a couple of inches taller than Aaron, with dark auburn hair and brownish hazel eyes. They both rocked the preppy look from middle school to present day.

"Okay, well…it's nice to have you home, *ma petite,*" Helene said, cracking open the door.

"*Maman,* wait," Jules called out.

"*Oui, ma petite bijou?*"

"Is my package up here?"

Helene pointed to a corner of the bedroom. Jules's eyes locked on the box addressed to her as her mother closed the door.

Her old bedroom was vaguely familiar. The only reason it could be considered her room now was because it was her room then. Her queen-size bed was still there, but now the walls were a deep purple instead of the pale pink color called Pixie Dust.

She opened the box that was waiting in the corner of her room, and as she expected, she found several individually wrapped presents. This was how she was going to spend her first night back in the room where she had spent her entire childhood and adolescence. At the bottom of her book bag, she found her fully charged portable vaporizer. Although it looked a little larger than a standard e-cigarette pen, it didn't look out of the ordinary. The best part was that the pen gave off no conspicuous smell. The tetrahydrocannabinol could be heated, inhaled, and enjoyed…even in public. Another plus was that the bowl was deep, so she didn't have to constantly fool with her weed or keep a lot of it on her. Jules wanted to make sure the vaporizer was good and hot so she could ease her anxiety immediately after she got what she needed out of the box.

The first present she opened was a medium-size, decorative wooden box. When she opened it, she found two ounces of her "relief." Jules pinched off a small piece and broke it apart between her fingers, put some in the vaporizer, and inhaled. "Ahhh," she exclaimed.

The next gift was a six-pack of knee-high socks with an ounce of weed in the toes. Leslie knew how much Jules didn't enjoy cold weather. After she retrieved the hidden presents from the socks, she noticed a shoe bag…a Prada shoe bag.

Leslie had bought herself a pair of taupe Prada sandals with three-inch heels. Although they were gorgeous, she'd only worn them once. Leslie liked flats—expensive and fabulous flats—but flats nonetheless. The three ounces in the Prada shoe bag put the count at eleven.

A small makeup bag containing a few of her favorite vegan cosmetics held two ounces too.

The last gift was in a rectangular box with a note on top that read:

> *Jewels, I enjoyed every moment we spent together and will forever cherish each memory I have of you (us). You're worth your weight in diamonds and gold, bébé. Todo mi amor para siempre, Javi.*

Javier was the man Jules had dated in Miami. They weren't together when she graduated, nor was he in the country right now. He'd given the presents to Leslie before he'd left.

A Rolex watch with a diamond bezel was fastened around a pair of pink lace panties that was neatly wrapped around another ounce of weed. The other ounce was wrapped in a pair of red lace panties, but this pair had a one-carat diamond bracelet set in white gold wrapped around it, holding the small package together. At the bottom of the box sat the ounce that completed the pound. So as of today, Jules had enough weed to last a whole year, comfortably, without her having to look for any. The realization put her mind at ease as she began to vape her second bowl while she unpacked a few items. At least the weed would increase her appetite and more than likely help her get through dinner with her parents and Lovey without incident.

After dinner Jules vaped again and lay down in bed. She found some soothing music on Pandora and got comfortable.

Everything is okay, she reminded herself. She closed her eyes and exhaled a steady mist. *The point is to be here for Lovey. Focus on Lovey, every day. Relax your jaws. No clenching;*

clenching doesn't make anything better. And breathe. She took a few more hits off the vaporizer and concentrated on the sounds of the harmonious instruments. Several minutes later, she was asleep, vaporizer in hand. One of its features was that it turned off every two minutes so it wouldn't waste the weed, and there'd also be no threat of Jules burning down the house. She had enough problems right now without worrying about that.

Chapter 2

*J*ules spent the next two weeks vaping constantly and keeping all of Lovey's appointments, both social and medical. She and Lovey were sitting at the dining-room table one night after Sunday dinner when her dad looked at his mother over the top of his glasses.

"What time does your day start tomorrow?" he asked.

"I have physical therapy at nine," Lovey replied, pushing a few loose gray tendrils out of her face. "Then we do some weight-bearing exercises and get into the pool. We should be done by one or so. Then I'll take a nap at two."

"Okay. Jules, I expect you at the office from nine to twelve thirty. Philip needs…" He trailed off for a moment. "Let's just say Philip could use your assistance, and I'll be grateful."

Jules just nodded as she twirled her long blond hair and thought, *Well, at least I can do all this stoned out of my brain.*

The next morning, after Jules had delivered Lovey to physical therapy a little early, she did as her father had told her and made her way to his office. She walked in through the back door just before the office opened at nine.

"Oh, thank God," Philip said. "I'm so happy to see you, Jules. I can't keep all the bills straight. The filing and the phones I've got, but the billing is so confusing."

"Good morning to you too. No worries. I got you, Philip. The bills are no problem. Where can I find them?"

Philip Dwyer was her dad's administrative assistant, but he looked like a TV anchorman; he was perfectly coiffed every day. Although Philip was taller than Jules, he was short for a man and had short, curly, brown hair and dark-brown eyes. He had worked at the law office for about a year and was quite efficient with clients as well as paperwork but terrible at crunching numbers.

Philip was answering the phone as he pointed to her dad's office. Jules opened the door and looked at the four stacks of paper on top of the solid oak desk. *This is going to take a while,* she thought. She sat down and opened the laptop that was on the desk. Just as she realized she didn't know any of the necessary usernames or passwords, the door opened and in walked Eli.

"I have those contracts for your sig—Juliana?" He looked confused and astonished and amazing. He was standing in front of her wearing a crisp white shirt with a deep-blue tie and gray pants. "When did you get back? What are you doing here?" He grinned wildly, his eyes shining their clear cerulean blue as he walked closer to her.

Eli King, born Elijah Shlomy King, was every fantasy Jules had ever had come to life. She had been in love with him since she was twelve and he was fifteen. And she wasn't the only one who loved him—he was loved and crushed on and had broken young hearts in at least three counties.

His father, Sam, was Jewish and a cardiologist, while his mother, Debra, was a black woman who had converted to Judaism and was the vice president of a bank. They had moved to Boston in the 1970s from Washington, DC. Eli was yummy all the way around for several reasons.

First of all, he was tall, standing at about six foot two, and his years of running track and participating in competitive swimming had sculpted his body to perfection. His diverse creation had given his skin the color of rich maple syrup, and his amazing hair looked great short or in a neat Afro. He was smart, funny, athletic, and just to make him completely and totally irresistible…he had those stunning blue eyes.

But he was her brother Chris's best friend. Eli also was friends with her other brother, Aaron, so during their childhood and adolescence he'd been off limits. And it was absolutely laughable to Jules that he could have any interest in her whatsoever. The girls Eli dated were model types and always seemed too pretty for real life, but that was kind of how Jules thought about Eli: too pretty for real life. During his senior year of high school, he had dated Miss Teen Massachusetts. He went to law school at Brown and currently worked for Jules's father as an all-purpose problem solver. Although Eli had been working there for just a few months, Thomas Dempsey trusted him implicitly. He was the firm's senior litigator, which allowed "Mr. D," as Eli called him, to concentrate on his priorities as a congressman.

Jules smiled back at Eli as he stood in the doorway, because if anyone could bring a smile to her lips, he could, but secretly she was panicking. Thank goodness the desk stood between them, and it worked in her favor that she was already sitting too. As soon as she saw him, her knees went weak and her legs shook. He wasn't someone she had expected to see, especially since they hadn't seen each other in many years. If Jules had to guess, she would've imagined him married to an exotic beauty, with a few gorgeous children to boot.

"It's just 'Jules' now. I got back two weeks ago. You know my Poppy died right?"

Eli nodded. "I'm really sorry. How's your grandma?"

"She's dealing. Lovey came to live with Ma and Dad, and now I'm a granny nanny, which basically means I'm her chauffeur extraordinaire, and while she's at physical therapy or socializing with her friends, I'll be here organizing the bills and helping Philip," she said, her heart slamming against her chest.

"So…you're back," he said with another grin.

"Yeah, I guess so. For now anyway. What about you? When did you move back to Boston?"

"Two years ago. After I passed the Massachusetts Bar, I spent three years traveling to several countries, teaching English in the Peace Corps. When I turned twenty-eight, I decided to come home. I've been working for your dad for a few months."

"You? Traveling the world, huh? That doesn't surprise me."

Just then Philip walked in, carrying another pile of papers with bills mixed throughout, and placed them on the desk.

"Your father just called. He won't be in until eleven," he told Jules, then turned around and walked out of the office.

Eli held up a stack of documents he had brought in. "Where can I put these so they won't be in your way?" he asked.

"What's wrong with your office, counselor?"

He thought for moment then said, "Well…nothing, but these contracts need your dad's signature. And I'm trying to get my desk cleaned off because fundraising for his next campaign will begin soon, and I'm trying to get a head start on my organizing."

"Okay…you heard Philip. He'll be in at eleven, so bring them back then. Besides, if you don't get out of here, I won't get anything done." Jules smiled up at him.

Eli reluctantly did as asked and walked out with the contracts, but as soon as he left, he turned around and walked right back into the office.

"Did you just shut me down and kick me out?" he said in his lawyer voice.

"Get out. You're a distraction," Jules said laughingly, trying to ignore the allure he had over her.

Every time he had looked at her since she was twelve years old, she had melted—*every time.* Most of her brothers' friends could be categorized by varying degrees of "asshole"—from tight sphincter to gaping hole—but not Eli. Certainly he could be; everybody can be an asshole. But he'd never been an asshole to Jules, not once. When they were teenagers, her feelings weren't conspicuous. She never would've been able to bear the embarrassment if someone had actually called her out on her crush. Her playful nature and quick wit always had helped her play off any remarks. "Who doesn't think he's cute?" she'd always say. And she only talked to Eli if he talked to her first, especially around his friends; he was older than her and always seemed to be surrounded by girls. Eli didn't dote on her or anything, but he didn't make her feel invisible either.

"I have to get some of this work done," Jules said, trying to sound stern.

Eli didn't push his luck and instead let her work. When Mr. Dempsey came in, he was pleasantly surprised to see Philip more at ease than he'd seen him in months. Jules appreciated the remark her dad made about Philip looking more relaxed then he'd seen him in months.

Around 12:15, Eli opened the door to his boss's office and saw Jules engulfed in her work. Her long blond bangs were swept away from her face, and he noticed her sweet, plump lips moving silently, as though she were counting or talking to herself. He didn't realize he was staring until Jules looked up through her piercing, chartreuse eyes and asked, "What do you need, Eli? Did you get those contracts signed?"

"Yes, they're done. I just wanted to know if you want to grab some lunch," Eli said casually. He hoped to conceal the eagerness in his voice, while Jules felt like a fifteen-year-old with a stomach full of butterflies. He rubbed his fingers against his clean-shaven chin.

"I can't," she said disappointedly. "I'm on Lovey duty. I have to leave in a few minutes to pick her up from physical therapy and take her home for lunch and a nap. I'm with her until six, when Ma comes home from volunteering at the food pantry."

"And then you're free after that?" Jules nodded as she began to gather her things. "Want to have dinner with me Thursday night?" he asked shyly.

"Why? Feel like you'll need some stimulating conversation after all the blank staring from your dates on Monday, Tuesday, and Wednesday?"

Eli closed his eyes and threw his head back as he put his hand over his heart and playfully said, "Ouch, Jules. That hurts. You really think I'm a man-whore?"

"Don't take it personally." She winked. "I think all men are."

"Oh, no, Ms. Dempsey. Let the record show that Thursday night is the first night I have free for dinner, since tonight I plan on working late then having dinner with my parents. Tuesday I'm taking care of my niece and nephew because it's my sister's anniversary. Wednesday night I'm having dinner with the client whose contracts your dad just signed. So as I previously stated, Thursday night is the first night I have free, and I'd like to take you to dinner."

"Yeah, okay," she said, the words falling out of her mouth while her brain was processing what was happening. She didn't sound anywhere near as excited as she actually was.

"Do you have any dietary restrictions we should plan for?"

Jules cocked her head to the side slightly, looking at him as if that were an odd question. "No…I like seafood, and I'll eat meat, but I don't have to, and I don't have any food allergies that I'm aware of. I'm not real crazy about Indian or Thai, but if you're absolutely dying for either, there are always one or two things I will eat."

Eli was delighted that Jules wasn't fussing about carbs or being gluten free or following the Paleo diet. They had eaten dinner together countless times during their childhood, sitting around her family's dining-room table, because he was practically family.

"And I don't particularly care to go downtown," she continued. "Being down here three days a week is enough."

"Sounds to me like you're avoiding something or somebody," Eli observed with his lawyer brain.

"I don't want to talk about it right now." Her voice trembled a bit as she snapped at him.

"Jules…what's up? I can't be on the lookout if I don't know what I'm looking for."

He sensed something was very wrong. Eli had been trained to listen to what people said and how they said it. He analyzed body language so frequently that he did it without thought; he could do it in a few languages too, but nonverbal cues were universal. Eli was incredibly intelligent, so much so that he had majored in psychology, along with political science, "for fun." And he would forever argue that his ability to read people made him a better lawyer. He knew when people were lying; hesitation spoke volumes.

She glared at him and said, "I'll be back Wednesday to continue my indentured servitude, so I'll see you then."

Eli wanted to keep Jules in his sight; he wanted her near him, and if that meant *not* talking about whatever she was avoiding, he would leave it alone for a while. He continued to be amazed that she was back in Boston. The few times he had asked Chris how she was doing or where she was living, he had given him short answers. "She's still in Miami. She's good," Chris would say. Reluctantly Eli would change the subject.

"So…this is going to be a regular thing then? You coming into the office?" Eli asked hopefully.

Jules was making her way out of her dad's office when she turned toward him and said, "Mostly Mondays and Wednesdays when Lovey has physical therapy, since I'll be downtown for three to four hours anyway…and it was a directive from the congressman himself. So fairly regularly, yes. And Philip seems beside himself with joy. All right, I have to get out of here. Later." Jules walked out after saying a quick good-bye to Philip.

The short commute to pick up Lovey wasn't long enough for Jules's overexcited nerves to calm down to a normal level, and she was trying to contain herself. She walked up the pathway and through the doors to the physical therapy center as she pushed her oversize sunglasses over her multicolored blond hair. Inside the building, she walked over to where Lovey was sitting and held out her hands to help her get up from the couch. Jules had two advantages: she was taller than Lovey and physically stronger.

Lovey looked up at her. "Who's got you beaming? You haven't looked like that since you got back here."

"You okay, Lovey? Maybe you need your glasses." Jules sidestepped around her grandma's comment.

Lovey's friend, Martha, said, "I need *my* glasses to see what color your hair is, girlie."

"Ms. Martha," Jules said, "my hair is really light, so my stylist puts warm brown and ginger lowlights in my hair to give it some dimension."

"Yeah, yeah, okay. I see it now. It looks better with my glasses on."

"Why, thank you, Ms. Martha. I'll tell my stylist you say so."

Once Jules and her grandmother were outside, Lovey was barely strapped into the passenger seat of Helene's BMW when she started again. "Did you have a lunch date or meet a handsome stranger?"

"No, Lovey. I smoked a bowl of weed before I came to get you"—she lied, but she was going to do that as soon as they got home—"and it made me super happy."

The next words out of Lovey's mouth stunned Jules.

"Could you roll me some of that weed? One of the physical therapists said it might help with my glaucoma."

A large smile crept across Jules's face. "Absolutely," she said, "and when you're 'good,' I'll make you anything you want for lunch."

"I'll have beef Wellington."

Jules laughed. "Pass. I've only eaten it once, and I definitely can't make it. How about grilled cheese with prosciutto and tomato?"

Lovely smiled. "Done."

When they got home, Lovey got washed up for lunch as Jules twisted some "relief" then walked into Lovey's room and sat on the bed.

"Inhale this just like a cigarette, but hold it in as long as you can," Jules instructed. "You'll probably only need to hit it a few times; it's some good shit." Lovey's eyes got big, but she smiled. "Pardon the expression," Jules continued. "Take it slow, and I'll come back in a few minutes to check on you."

"You're not staying?"

Jules smiled. "I don't mind supplying you and getting you 'good' every day, especially since it'll ease your arthritis and glaucoma, and it'll make you crazy hungry. But if you get caught, my dad is a lot less likely to yell at you than he is to yell at me, so I'll leave you to it. I'll be back in a few minutes. Holla if you need me."

About four hits and ten minutes later, Lovey's head was numb.

"I've never felt like this." Lovey looked up at Jules as she came back in the room.

"You okay, Lovey?" Jules was almost worried.

"I'm better than okay, honey."

"What do you feel like?"

"My joints don't hurt," she said, stretching and flexing her fingers. "And my eyes feel more normal than they have in years. They usually feel like hardboiled eggs from all the pressure." She giggled. "And I feel like I'm floating."

"That's it, Lovey—you're high. The more you do it, the better it gets."

Twenty minutes later, Lovey wanted that grilled cheese with prosciutto and tomato, along with a glass of orange juice. Shortly after she was finished eating, it was nap time. While Lovey was asleep, Jules packed a bowl and put her feet up as she lay back in the leather recliner in her room.

Those cerulean-blue eyes were all she could see—and his smile. Eli smiled at her every time he looked at her. At least that's what Jules thought. *I must be imagining things. And after all these years, he looks even better than I remember. How's that possible? And he wants to have dinner with me!* Her pulse quickened at just the thought of him. Eli always had been nice to her, so this wasn't any different, right?

After her nap, Lovey hit the joint four or five more times and left the window open for a while, until Jules knocked at the door.

"You up, Lovey?" she said, as she walked into the room.

Lovey was sitting on the couch, and she patted the spot beside her. Jules sat down as her grandmother said, "You were right, girlie…That's some good shit." They both laughed hysterically.

"We're going to have to get you a vaporizer if you want to continue, because I could smell it down stairs," Jules said. "Don't worry—I opened all the windows and turned the air off and all the fans on. It should clear out in ten or fifteen minutes. The vaporizer smells, but not like marijuana. I got one when I knew I was coming back to Boston. I knew being here was going to require an enormous amount of weed, which I'm happy to share by the way."

Lovey smiled at her granddaughter. "I know it was hard for you to come back, honey. I'm old, but not senile, and I have a long memory."

"No worries, Lovey. If there's anyone I'd come back for, it's you." Jules got up and helped her grandmother change her clothes and make her way downstairs.

"Hello! I'm home," Helene called out.

"We're in the kitchen, dear," Lovey said. Helene headed to the kitchen, where Lovey and Jules were starting dinner.

Helene had struggled with empty nest syndrome ever since Jules had left for Miami a decade ago. Since then, she had become involved in the community, volunteered at church, and taken some gardening and life-drawing classes. Right now she was also doing charity work at a food pantry and for an organization that delivered meals to homebound senior citizens. Along with that, soon she would be campaigning nonstop for the congressman. That was the entire reason Jules had to come back. Helene couldn't just drop her activities to care for Lovey; people depended on her to do the things she'd been doing since her daughter had left for college.

"You'll never guess who I ran into today, Jules," Helene chirped as she informed them about her day. She and her best friend, Violet, helped more than fifty elderly folks two or three days a week.

"Who was that, Ma?" Jules asked curiously, while wiping down the counter.

"Nancy Griffin, Denny and Danny's mom," Helene continued, as Jules stopped what she was doing. "She can be so braggy. Apparently Denny was just made a junior partner at O'Shea and Moore."

Lovey looked at Jules, who looked faint.

Shit! Shit! Shit! Denny Griffin was in fact in Boston and seemed to be doing well. This knowledge could be good, though. How could she use it to her advantage? She now knew where he worked so she'd know which general area to avoid. The terrifying part was that O'Shea and Moore was only about five blocks from her dad's law office. Jules wished she could just disappear.

Helene continued talking because she didn't know that the mere mention of Denny's name made Jules nauseous and angry. Her parents had no idea it was Denny who had traumatized their daughter all those years ago. Only a small group of people knew: Jules, Javier, Leslie, Jackie, Dr. Seda, and Denny. Thankfully Helene had moved on past Nancy Griffin and her bragging. The baked pasta in the oven was cooking, and Jules was preparing the salad as her father walked through the door.

"Hey, Ma," he said in Lovey's direction as he walked past Jules. He sidled up to Helene and kissed her on the lips as she tended to the asparagus.

"Hi, honey," Helene said, as her husband sampled some of the delicious food Jules and his wife were preparing. "Hey! Hands off the food, Tommy. Dinner will be ready in about twenty minutes," she scolded playfully.

"But I'm hungry now, my darling."

"Don't whine, son. Nobody likes it," Lovey said, as Thomas frowned.

The familiar banter made Jules feel safe somehow. Thomas went through the events of his day then asked the ladies about theirs. The tightening in Jules's chest was releasing a little as the conversation continued. Her ma hadn't said anything else about the spawn of Satan making junior partner. Maybe Helene figured Thomas already knew. In the midst of their conversation, the doorbell rang.

"Who could that be?" Helene wondered.

"I'll get it," Jules said, as her dad made his way upstairs to change his clothes.

Jules walked toward the front door then peeked out the window to see Eli standing there. His deep-blue tie was loosened, and his top shirt button was undone—even his Adam's apple was sexy. A courier bag was draped across the defined muscles of his chest.

"Hey, Eli. I thought you were working late and having dinner with your parents." Jules grinned as she opened the front door and gestured for him to come inside. She was wearing a hot-pink tank top with a built-in bra that showcased her full, perky, B-cup-size breasts, along with a pair of black sleep shorts that barely covered her delicious, round bottom.

Eli's throat went dry as he tried to clear it to speak. The gorgeous woman welcoming him into the house made him momentarily speechless. Whenever he'd thought about Jules, he hadn't taken into account that her body had fully developed in the last ten years. He hadn't planned on being taunted with her voluptuous figure when he had decided to stop by. Eli was nearly a foot taller than Jules's petite five-foot-three-inch frame; this tiny woman was torturing him, and she didn't have the slightest inkling.

Towering over her, he said, "Well smarty-pants, I just left the office, and I'm on my way to my parents' house. Your house is on the way, remember?" Eli's parents lived two blocks behind the Dempsey family. "I have some files that your pops is waiting for. And since I'm on my way over to my parents' house, I figured I'd drop them by."

Shrugging, Jules closed the door behind Eli and led him toward the kitchen, where he was received with warm greetings.

"Have a seat, Eli. Tommy will be down in just a few minutes. Are you hungry? Dinner is almost ready," Helene offered.

"Oh, no. Thanks, Mama D, but I'm on my way to have dinner with my parents. I just need to get these to Mr. D; he's been expecting them." Eli talked to the Dempsey family for a few more minutes while their dinner finished cooking.

As Jules showed Eli out, he said, "I forgot to get your phone number earlier. Can I have it?"

"You know the house number, don't you?" Jules said.

"Yes, but I don't have your cell number, unless you have the same number from eight years ago."

"It's the same as my dad's, but the last two digits are three two."

"That's easy. Thanks, Jules," he said, as he put her number into his contacts.

"Bye, Eli. Enjoy dinner with your parents."

"Bye, Jules. You too." She closed the front door behind him.

After Eli left for his parents' house and Jules joined her mother and grandmother in the kitchen, Lovey asked, "Does he usually make house calls?"

Helene looked up. "It's not unusual. Why?"

"Let's just say I don't think those files were what brought him here," she said with a mischievous grin as she looked straight at Jules.

Chapter 3

Wednesday morning

Two days later, when Eli got to the office, Jules wasn't there yet, and he felt something he'd been tamping down for a long time: disappointment.

"Don't make that sad face at me," Philip goaded.

Eli gave him half a smile. "'Morning, Philip," he said, as he put a cup of coffee on the front desk and carried the other two to his office.

Fifteen minutes later, Jules walked through the door and smiled at Philip as she was putting her phone in her bag.

"Our senior litigator brought coffee for you," Philip said with a smirk.

"Don't start with me. It's too early, Philip."

"Honey, he brought *me* coffee to cover for the fact that he brought *you* coffee."

"Maybe he brought us *both* coffee so he wouldn't seem rude," she shot back.

"That one"—Philip looked in the direction of Eli's office—"has no qualms about being rude. He might be gorgeous and charming, but he can be ruthless."

"Be nice," Jules said playfully, as she retrieved the bills from the elaborate oak shelves behind him.

Jules seemed to be in her own little world because she didn't hear Eli come up behind her. As she turned around, they collided, but he managed not to spill any coffee on either of them. The carpeted floor, however, didn't fare as well.

"Whoa!" Jules nearly screamed. "Nice save!"

"Yeah, except now your coffee is on the floor," Eli said, making a face while Philip came to the rescue with paper towels.

"Thanks," Jules told him, "but I never touch the stuff." Eli made that face again. "Caffeine affects me like I imagine crack or meth would. Sometimes I drink a Coke or sweet tea but never coffee."

"I never would've made it through college or law school without it," Eli replied.

"The taste never really appealed to me. Besides, I have different ways of easing myself into the morning. During undergrad I worked at night and took late-morning and afternoon classes. I'm not much of a morning person."

"Yeah, I think I remember you being a late sleeper." Eli looked like he was relishing a memory. He did remember. He remembered everything—or at least the things he wanted to remember. Jules was six when she broke her left arm; she fell out of a tree as she tried to keep up with the boys. Eli ran and got his dad, the doctor. As a child, Jules was a dancer: tap, jazz, ballet, pointe, and hip-hop. At age fourteen, she had a solo *en pointe* with the Boston Ballet Company. Eli had agreed to go to the performance to keep Chris company. Chris had called it a "dance thing." Although they both complained a bit, as seventeen-year-old boys do, Eli was captivated. From that night on, he saw Jules differently. He'd always remember the way she looked in that light-pink sundress the summer after the ballet too. What Eli couldn't seem to remember now was the last time he had seen Jules before Monday morning. Hell, he was sure it was before she started going by "Jules."

Eli bent down and used the wet paper towels Philip had brought over to blot up the mess, and then he used the dry towels to finish. Philip was standing there with the trash can.

"Thank you, Philip," Eli said in a singsong voice as Philip walked in the opposite direction to empty the trash.

"Did you figure out where you want to eat tomorrow night?" Eli asked Jules.

"Oh, I didn't know I was supposed to pick," she said, staring at him intently. "You're the one who lives here. Where do you like to go?"

"Well, it depends. Do you want fancy dinner or casual dining?"

"Nothing fancy. I've unpacked next to nothing and have no idea where my fancy clothes are."

"You've been here more than two weeks and you haven't unpacked? C'mon Jules, you have to unpack. What if I wanted to take you out to the Ritz?"

Jules chuckled. "I know—I can't keep living out of boxes. I guess I just didn't want to admit to myself that I'm here to stay for a while. Maybe I'll unpack during Lovey's nap today. What time are you coming to get me tomorrow night?"

"You said your mom would be home about seven, right?"

"Six," Jules said with a smile.

"Okay, let's split the difference. I'll see you at six thirty."

"Six thirty it is then." She smiled again. "Now get out so I can work," she said, attempting to sound stern. Eli looked a little hurt. "Don't look at me like that, Eli. You're a distraction. And I need to try to make a dent in all this before I go get Lovey."

"Yeah, yeah. So…I guess you can't go out to lunch?"

Jules shook her head. "Nope, sorry. Not today, but you'll have me all to yourself at six thirty tomorrow night. Now out," she said without looking up at him.

"Don't work that pretty little head of yours too hard," Eli replied as he strode out of Thomas Dempsey's office.

Did he just call me pretty? Jules thought. *I must be trippin'.*

⟡

The next morning, Jules and Lovey piled into Helene's BMW for the forty-minute drive to the farmers' market. The sun was barely up, and Jules and Lovey were "in the clouds." Lovey, Mary Katherine Dempsey, never had been one to hold her tongue, but the weed made her comments flow even more freely. As Jules pulled onto the highway, Lovey said, "What are your plans after we're finished here?"

"I don't know. I figured by the time we got back, you'd be ready for lunch. Then maybe you'd want to take a nap because this heat can be exhausting."

"That's not what I mean. What are your plans after I'm gone?" Lovey asked.

"Lovey, don't talk like that. I don't want to think about it." Jules was short.

"Well, it doesn't matter if you want to think about it. It'll come someday, and I'm hoping for sooner rather than later.

I'm old, and life is tiring, and my Joe is waiting for me," Lovey said sweetly. "So tell me, what are your plans?"

"New York. I'm going to New York. When I was in Miami, I did some consulting for a woman named Annette Young, and we became good friends. She owns a property group that manages eighty properties around the world. She splits her time between New York and Miami, but she spends most of her time in Miami, and she wants me in New York."

"The city, huh? That sounds exciting. Have you found a place to live yet?"

"Actually I met with Annette's realtor," Jules said, "and she showed me a few places the last time I traveled with Annette to New York, but it's way too early to start looking to buy something. I've been saving over the last eight years or so and have almost thirty grand in the bank, but that's nowhere near what I need for a down payment."

As they pulled into the parking lot at the farmers' market, Lovey said, "I want you to find a place soon, and don't worry about the down-payment money." Jules looked at Lovey out of the corner of her eye, but the old woman didn't miss a thing.

"Don't dismiss me, young lady. You have no idea what I have stashed away. And after everything you're doing for me, I need the peace of mind that you're safe and living in a good place. I also want to see the place before I'm gone, so hop to it."

"All right, Lovey," Jules said. "And thank you. I'll text Annette while you're endlessly picking through the produce." She knew better than to argue with her grandmother.

"I don't like bruised fruits and vegetables or smashed bread," Lovey declared.

"Right. No one *likes* bruised produce or smashed bread, but I could write Annette a short story in the time it'll take you to decide on things. It's okay if the bread is smashed a little, Lovey. We're going to eat it," Jules said, smiling.

"Well, in that novel you write to Annette, tell her the place has to be in a good neighborhood and close to work, maybe the Upper West Side."

"All right, Lovey. Now let's get some good stuff before it gets too crowded…or too hot."

After Jules texted Annette, they purchased an incredible amount of fresh fruit and vegetables. The peaches and strawberries looked particularly inviting. While Lovey was picking through the various fruit, Jules went and found the fresh baked goods for the ride home. She surprised Lovey with a dozen baklava bites and four pecan sticky buns.

"Your ma is going to be so happy about all this fresh produce," Lovey said. "I know she has quite a few dishes planned for this food."

"Did you get everything on the list? That has to be everything," Jules said.

"The only thing I can't seem to find is gingerroot."

"Ma will live without it. Let's get out of here. It's barely ten thirty, and I'm already sweating, so I know you must be hot." She paused in thought for a moment then said, "Wait right here. I'm going to get us a couple of bottles of water to wash down these sweets on the ride home."

When Jules returned with the water, she helped Lovey into the car. As Lovey got herself situated, she asked, "You have anything for the ride home?"

Jules smiled. "I do, but it's in the vaporizer."

"Well, that's okay. I need to learn how to use it anyway."

Jules and Lovey got high on the way home, and by the time they arrived, Lovey was ready for a snack and a nap.

Jules decided to get into the shower so it would be one less thing for her to do later. She didn't hear her phone ring while she was in there, and it took a few minutes for her to check it once she was out.

She'd gotten a text from Eli: *See you soon.*

Jules text Eli back, *Don't tell me you're thinking about food already...LOL.*

He replied: *Nope, I'm not thinking about the food.*

The anticipation was nearly too much, but Jules just wouldn't let herself see the hints Eli was dropping. She knew she had to be reading too much into their recent interactions. Although the two of them always had been friends, all those old crush feelings had come rushing back the instant their eyes had met four days ago. But those feelings weren't "crush" feelings anymore. When Jules was a teenager, she knew she was in love with Eli, and she was more in love with him now. She wasn't even sure she would be able to make it through dinner without making a complete idiot of herself. The vaporizer was hot now, and she was calming herself down as she put on her makeup.

Lovey knocked on the door then poked her head inside the room. "What are you doing, honey?"

Jules was sitting on her bed, applying some lipstick. "I'm getting ready. I'm going out to dinner with Eli later."

"Is he the young man who stopped by the other night?" Lovey inquired.

"You know he is, Lovey. Why do you ask?" Jules looked at her between inhaling from the vaporizer and coating her thick lashes with black mascara.

"No reason," Lovey said, trying to sound innocent. "I just think he likes what he sees."

Jules shook her head. "You're talking nonsense. I think he's just trying to help with my transition back to Boston, whether he knows it or not. Eli and I have been friends for more than half my life."

"Sometimes, girlie, friends make the *best* lovers." Lovey nearly blushed as Jules tried to dismiss the statement, trying not to get her hopes up too high.

Several minutes after six, the doorbell rang. Jules was wearing a bathrobe, and her hair was pulled up in hot rollers on the top of her head as she made her way to answer it. She opened the door to find Eli standing there in a bright-blue button-down shirt with the sleeves rolled up twice, no tie, and relaxed-fit khakis.

"Hey, you're early…You must be hungry. I'm almost ready," Jules said. If the thought had even entered her mind that this was anything close to a date, she'd have been mortified that she had answered the door this way. Jules just thought they were two friends having dinner together.

Eli smiled coyly at her, his blue eyes more intense with the complementary color of his shirt.

"You can come upstairs," Jules said. "Lovey's been keeping me company while I'm getting ready." Eli followed her to her room, where Lovey was sitting in the recliner.

"Jules, I didn't know you were having company," Lovey said.

"You didn't tell Lovey we were having dinner?" Eli looked at Jules quizzically. "Are you ashamed to be seen with me?" he said facetiously. "It also looks like you've done some unpacking, unless you shoved all the boxes into your closet."

Jules looked at Lovey and Eli in disbelief. "No, I unpacked. Are you two in on this together? Are you both trying to drive me crazy?" she asked, walking into the small walk-in closet to change into a dress.

"Where are you taking my granddaughter for dinner, young man?" Lovey asked Eli.

"Federico's. It's a little Italian spot off the beaten path. It's authentic, and Federico, the owner, sings during dessert," Eli said. "Tomorrow night some friends and I are going to a bar to watch a Red Sox game. You think she'll want to go with me?"

"It's up to you to ask," Lovey replied, "but if she says yes, you can't leave her alone."

Jules walked out of the walk-in closet wearing a kelly-green sundress that crossed tightly against her perky breasts. The dress fit her body so well that she didn't need a bra. While Eli and Lovey continued talking, Jules walked into the bathroom to take the rollers out of her hair. The contrast between the lowlights and highlights in her hair, her porcelain skin, and her piercing green eyes had Eli stealing glances at her so as not to stare.

"Are you ready?" Eli asked as Jules ran her fingers through her curls.

"We can go when Ma gets home," Jules replied, looking for a suitable pair of shoes.

"Nonsense," Lovey interjected. "Don't let me stop you."

Jules shook her head. "You're kidding, right? Do you have any idea how ridiculously pissed my parents would be if they came home and found you alone? No, thank you! That's a confrontation I'm more than patient enough to avoid."

Lovey glared at her granddaughter, but before she could say anything, Jules flashed a smile at them both and said,

"Let's go downstairs and get dinner started. You know you're hungry, Lovey."

Twenty minutes later, Helene walked into the kitchen to find Jules standing at the stove making dinner while Eli and Lovey talked and prepped some fruits and veggies.

"Well, what's going on in here?" Helene asked.

"Lovey was ready for dinner, so I started it while we were waiting for you to come home so Eli and I could go."

Helene looked puzzled. "Go? Where are you two going?"

"Out to dinner. I'll be home later," Jules said, as she kissed her ma on the cheek and grabbed her purse.

"Eli," Helene called out, "take care of my baby."

"You know I will," Eli replied.

Chapter 4

The car ride to Federico's was a bit awkward. Jules could *feel* Eli's eyes on her. She tried really hard not to notice, not to be awkward, but it was difficult. Suddenly neither of them could think of anything to talk about.

"I'm hoping you actually did pick a place for us to eat," Jules finally said.

"No, I just thought we'd ride around aimlessly until hunger overtook us," Eli said with a light laugh.

"Eli…" Jules snipped.

"Calm down. Come on, Jules…be logical," Eli said. "Do you think I'd get you out on a date without making dinner plans?"

"A date, huh?" Jules wondered aloud.

"Of course it's a date. You're wearing an amazing dress; I picked you up; and we're going to dinner. It's a date."

"For more than half my life, I thought I was off limits to any male who knew Aaron and Chris. That was according to the Neanderthals who pose as my older brothers," Jules shot back. "Isn't there some kind of 'bro code' you're violating? Are you trying to challenge that?"

"I think I already did. Here we are, right?" Eli smiled at her, and true to form, Jules's insides melted. "Besides, Chris and Aaron have families now and live in New Hampshire.

They have lives of their own, and we're adults now. We don't need their permission to go out to dinner…or to date for that matter."

Holy. Fucking. Shit, Jules thought. *Say what?*

Eli pulled into the parking lot of Federico's. It wasn't downtown, just like she'd asked. As Eli turned off the ignition, Jules took a look at the small restaurant.

She smiled. "Italian. Good choice."

"I'm glad you approve," Eli said, chuckling.

When they walked inside, Federico's wife, Carmella, a short, round woman in her fifties, greeted them. She led them through the scattered patrons toward the back right of the dimly lit room and seated them in a two-person booth. Their legs were going to touch; it was inevitable. Eli was more than six feet tall. Jules was actively thinking about this and planned on rolling with it. Once they were comfortably seated and looking at the menu, she crossed her legs and lightly placed her right foot somewhere behind one of his calves. Eli didn't move, and neither did she, but she definitely caught him off guard.

"What are you having?" Eli asked.

"How's the eggplant parm?" Jules wondered.

"I don't know. I've never had it here, and I don't think I like eggplant." Eli made a face.

"Have you ever tried it?" she inquired.

"A couple of times, but I didn't care for it."

"The marinara helps, and the eggplant is usually baked and crusted with Parmesan and other cheeses. It's delicious. I'd also like either the Chianti or the '98 Shiraz—you choose. A house salad, a cup of minestrone, and eggplant parmesan," Jules said, as she continued to peruse the menu. "What about you?" She looked up at Eli, who seemed lost in thought as he stared at her.

"The fettuccine Alfredo is amazing. It has sweet peas, broccoli, and lobster in it."

"I guess that means we're sharing, or at least you'll have to let me have a bite or two," Jules said with a grin.

Dinner passed with light conversation about the past ten years. Eli told Jules stories about his travels to various countries around the world. She did all she could to keep him talking. She asked him questions and continued the conversation with comical stories from Miami. And Eli happily shared his fettuccine Alfredo and even tried the eggplant Parmesan.

The ride home was a bit more intense, thanks to the two bottles of Shiraz. The saying "A drunk man's words are a sober man's truth," aptly described the situation. Eli, with his excellent memory, wasn't purposely trying to manipulate Jules, but he did want to know why she didn't want to go downtown or be back in Boston for that matter.

"Hey, tomorrow night some guys I play pickup games with are meeting at Dunleavy's to watch the Red Sox play the Braves. You want to go?"

Jules looked at him. "To Dunleavy's?"

"Yes…Dunleavy's."

"That's downtown, right?" Eli nodded. "I really don't want to go out downtown." She was adamant.

"You told me that already. I'll be there the entire time. What's the problem?" he probed.

"Eli, I had a nice time tonight, and I don't want to ruin it by telling you why I don't want to go downtown. That's a conversation for another time."

"Oh, no, you don't. You forget that I know you. You're going to construct the story with the least amount of details so it sounds like you're answering my questions, but you're really not. What's got you freaking out?"

He stopped at a red light. Jules didn't say a word. Eli was right; he did know Jules in every way but one. He had seen her experience laughter and tears and just about every emotion in between. Since she was his best friend's little sister, she always had been around—not necessarily in the foreground but around. They had attended the same schools, the same parties, and from third grade through high school, Eli practically had lived at their house for half the week, while Chris was at his house the other half.

Eli was the only boy in the King family and the baby brother of two older sisters, Sasha and Talia. Sasha was the oldest and still lived in Boston. She had two children under the age of five. She was a radiologist, and her husband, Garrett, was urologist. Talia lived with her three children and husband, Nate, just outside of Boston in Waltham. She and her husband owned a small IT company and did computer repairs of all kinds: hardware, software, and mechanical.

Eli's mom loved having Chris over because he was so well mannered. Debra, Eli's mother, and Helene had become fast friends due to the strong bond of their sons. And they both lived with the belief that "it takes a village," so they never had minded hosting each other's child.

Jules sighed. "I'll tell you tomorrow night after we leave the bar."

"I'm going to hold you to that. Are you coming into the office tomorrow?"

She shook her head. "Lovey has water therapy and water aerobics tomorrow, so I'm going to swim some laps and hopefully work off some of my nervous energy."

Eli pulled his dark-gray Land Rover up to the curb in front of the Dempsey residence and shut off the engine. He looked as if he wanted to say something but was struggling to find the right words.

"Thanks for dinner," Jules said, breaking the silence. "I had a really nice time."

She opened the door and got out. Eli did the same.

"What are you doing?" she asked.

"Walking you to the door. I always walk my date to the door," Eli said, following her to the porch.

"Even the next morning?" Jules quipped.

"Ouch! Jules, you're killing me. You missed your calling as a comedienne, you know."

"Don't mind me. That might be a touch of jealousy talking."

"What's that?" Eli's ears perked up.

"Nothing," she muttered.

She turned around on the step above him and pressed her lips to his. His hands went to her hips, but before he could return the kiss, she pulled her head back, wiped a smudge of lip gloss from his lips, and said, "Good night, Eli. Text me when you get home."

Fifteen minutes later, Eli texted Jules and thanked her for her company. She responded by thanking him once again. He replied, *Sweet dreams,* and she replied, *You too.*

Chapter 5

*L*ovey got into the warm, three-foot-deep therapy pool near the entrance to the large pool area at the Commonwealth Sports Club. It was an indoor pool where lots of seniors participated in water therapy. Jules stretched and did some breathing exercises for twenty minutes then dove in, not even noticing that Eli was walking out of the men's locker room. He dove in behind her and let the cool water soothe the heat that was radiating from his body. Eli hadn't been able to put any logical thoughts together, much less get any sleep, since Jules had pressed her lips to his. When Jules reached the wall on the opposite end of the pool, she came up and exhaled. Eli emerged from the water behind her, startling her.

"Oh, shit! Eli, what the hell are you doing?" Jules gasped.

Eli moved closer to her and pushed his body into hers and her body into the wall. "I wanted to see you this morning."

Before she could respond, he kissed her full on, and she returned in kind. Thankfully the traffic in the pool was light, and no one was paying them any attention. Lovey was at the other end of the facility in the warm therapy pool, so she couldn't see them—if she had, she never would have let this go. When Jules broke her lips away from Eli's, he saw the confusion in her eyes.

"I couldn't believe you kissed me last night, but I wanted a *real* kiss," he said with a sly smile. "You kissed me like we were five."

"Eli, I've known you for more of my life than I haven't. I didn't want to make your head explode," Jules said, smiling.

Eli kissed Jules again, sweetly but purposefully, as she wrapped her arms around his neck. He used his left hand to hold them against the side of the pool then wrapped his right arm around her waist and pressed their bodies together tightly. Their lips and tongues moved together as if they'd kissed a thousand times before. This was a public display of affection in a very public place, but at the moment they were alone at the far end of the Olympic-size pool. Jules lightly sucked on Eli's bottom lip then took her lips away. She was fighting every urge to wrap her legs around his waist. She pulled him into an embrace so her lips were next to his left ear.

"You'll be late for work if you don't go soon," Jules said. "And if you're late for work, you'll have to work late, and then we'll be late to the bar."

"The game starts at six, I think," Eli replied, still holding their bodies against the wall. "Besides, I didn't think you were too happy about going to the bar."

"I'm going to the bar so you'll shut up about it already. Call me when you're on your way over. Now go—you're distracting me."

"How am I distracting you?" he asked, kissing her neck and laughing.

"Seriously, Eli. You exist—therefore you distract me. Now isn't the time to play dumb. I need to restore my thought processes back to normal, and I can't with you doing *that*."

"All right," he said reluctantly. "See you this evening," He gave her a quick kiss good-bye, then swam back to the other end of the pool.

Helene walked through the front door at quarter to six. Lovey was sitting in the living room, knitting a multicolored blanket. *Judge Judy* was on the TV.

"Something smells delicious," Helene said to Lovey as she sat down beside her.

"My granddaughter made lasagna and garlic bread. She finely sliced some vegetables and put in about half the meat. She also used plain Greek yogurt with some cottage cheese and a really good Parmesan instead of all those heavy cheeses. If you don't tell Thomas, I doubt he'll notice it's pretty healthy."

"Where is Jules?"

"Upstairs, getting ready to go out with Eli again."

Helene smiled slyly. "Is that so?"

"Yes." Lovey smiled too. "They're just meeting some people at a bar to watch the Red Sox, but I think it's great."

Helene sighed. "It is. She's been in love with him forever."

She walked upstairs to find Jules sliding into a pair of snug low-rise jeans torn at the knee. The University of Miami baseball T-shirt hugged her curves. Her makeup usually consisted of tinted moisturizer, a mascara that thickened her lashes, and lip gloss in any of the various Juicy Tube flavors.

"*Ma petite bijou,* you look beautiful," Helene complimented her daughter.

Jules smiled. "*Merci beaucoup, Maman.* But I still think you have to say that because you're my ma."

"Oh, no, no. Thankfully you look just like your *mémère.* My mama was so beautiful. You, *ma petite bijou,* have her natural beauty…and her lovely green eyes."

"You say that as though you're a ghastly sight, Ma. You favor Mém, so I must look like you, but you look like Papa too."

Although Jules and Helene were both petite, Helene was a bit taller. Helene had hazel eyes and gray hair that was colored and highlighted every four weeks to give the appearance of blond hair.

"I really look like my father's mother," she said, "but you're right—I do favor Mém. *Merci, ma petite bijou.*"

"No need to thank me, Ma. It's true. You seem to have aged better than Mém. I hope I age as well as you have," Jules said, as she used her fingers to comb through her hair, which she'd once again curled with hot rollers.

"So are you excited to be going out with Eli?"

"I don't think it's quite like that, Ma."

"Don't be so sure, *jeune fille.*"

Jules shrugged. "Just don't get your hopes up."

⸝⸝⸝⸝

Eli texted Jules at ten minutes to six: *I'm leaving the office now. See you in fifteen.*

You're not going home first? Jules texted back.

No, we're already going to miss the beginning of the game.

Okay. Don't text and drive. See you when you get here. I'm almost ready.

Jules put a Juicy Tube in her pocket and grabbed her driver's license and $40 in cash. As she put her ID and money in her back pocket and rolled up the bottom of her jeans, she noticed how badly she needed a pedicure. Looking at her unkempt feet made her get a pair of thin ankle socks and look for her Nike Air Maxes. As she was digging through her closet, searching for her pair of green, orange, and white sneakers, her phone sounded again.

It was another text from Eli: *I can't remember the last time I saw you.*

This morning in the pool, silly, Jules texted back. *And you'd better not be texting and driving.*

I'm at a red light, smartass, and I meant before you came back to Boston.

Probably sometime during the summer before your senior of college.

Jules put on her socks and sneakers. The vaporizer was hot and ready. She took ten minutes to "get right." Then she brushed her teeth and pumped two light sprays of Burberry Brit Sheer. At least now her nerves were eased, and she *looked* like she was ready to enjoy herself.

Her phone sounded again: *Come downstairs.*

Jules took one last look in the mirror then headed downstairs. Eli was sitting in the front room on the couch with Helene and Lovey.

"You have tomorrow morning off, *ma petite*. Lovey is having lunch with Martha at noon. You should be home by eleven a.m., *oui?*" Helene asked.

Jules' eyes almost popped out of her head at her mother's insinuation. Helene was smiling at Jules.

"Oui, Maman," Jules said, trying desperately not to be embarrassed. She kissed Helene and Lovey on the cheek and wished them a good evening.

"Oh, and Eli…" Helene said.

"Yes, Mama D?"

"Take care of my baby."

"You know I will," Eli replied nervously.

"She can always make me feel like I'm fifteen," Jules said, once they were outside and walking to the car.

"Your curfew was eleven a.m. when you were fifteen?" Eli mused.

"No. It's just that I'm practically grown, and she still manages to embarrass me."

"Why do you feel embarrassed?" Eli asked pointedly as he opened the passenger-side door for her.

"Because I'm standing in my parents' living room, with you, about to go out, and my mother all but paints a picture and directs me not to come home until tomorrow."

"So don't disappoint her." Eli grinned devilishly as he backed out of the driveway.

"Wouldn't you just love that?" Jules said sarcastically.

"I'm going to let that go for now," Eli said, turning up the radio to ponder that thought.

Jules met three interesting, likable young men who played basketball with Eli. Patty (Patrick), a Boston-born Irish kid of average height, was a sous chef at a popular seafood restaurant.

Brian, a handsome short black man from Seattle, was a resident at Mass General, training to be an oncologist. Johnny, a law student from Michigan, was a clerk at the Suffolk County Municipal Court.

Each of the men bought Jules a beer. After she finished her third Sam Adams, her buzz was stronger than she'd expected. The guys teased her about nursing those three beers, but there was no way she could have kept up with them. Drinking definitely wasn't her thing.

"I have to use the ladies' room," she said, as she pushed her chair away from the table.

"Don't be gone too long in there, U of M. You're the prettiest woman I've seen all week," Brian called after her. He turned to Eli. "What? Don't look at me like that. I've been on ER rotation, and the patients and my interns require great personalities for me to even tolerate them. I'm not trying to bang any of them, but at least give me something to look at."

"Where have you been hiding this one?" Johnny asked Eli.

"Nowhere," Eli responded. "She's my best friend's little sister."

"She don't look so little anymore," Patty chimed in.

They all laughed and nodded in agreement. The game was on commercial break as a small crowd moved past them. Eli turned toward the table to get his beer, and when he turned back around, he came face-to-face with Denny Griffin.

To an unknowing, unsuspecting female, Denny Griffin was an attractive man. His round light-brown eyes complemented his dark-brown hair. Denny looked like a guy you'd see in a generic clothing ad—he just looked like he belonged—but he was much cuter when he was younger. He wasn't unattractive; he was just better looking earlier in life.

"Hey, man. How's it going?" Denny asked, as he extended his hand to shake hands with a puzzled Eli.

"It's all good, man. How are you?" Eli responded, unable to place whom he was talking to. When Denny noticed Eli didn't seem to recognize him, he said, "Dennis Griffin, Danny's older brother.'"

Then it clicked, and Eli said, "Oh, right. Hey, Denny. Good to see you. What are you up to these days?"

"Living the dream, man. Working, fucking, playing, just doing whatever the hell I want. I've been with O'Shea and Moore for almost eight years now, just made junior partner. Things are going well."

Before Eli could respond, the Red Sox player on second was trying to steal third, and the bar crowd was going nuts. As the roar began to die down, Denny looked over at Eli and said, "Some people are waiting for me. It was good to see you. Tell Juliana she looks great." He walked to the back of the bar, away from the bathrooms, and toward the table where his friends were sitting. Eli didn't think much of their encounter, other than the fact that Denny had called her "Juliana" instead of "Jules."

"Who was that?" Johnny asked.

"A guy from my old neighborhood," Eli replied.

A few minutes later, Jules returned from the restroom. The guys continued to talk as they watched the game. When Jules asked for a glass of water, Eli asked if she was ready to go. It was the bottom of the sixth inning, and Atlanta was struggling. It was three to one, Boston.

"Actually, yeah, I'd like to go if that's okay," Jules said.

"All right, guys, we're out of here," Eli said to a few resounding protests.

"Good night. It was nice to meet all of you," Jules said as they stood up to leave.

Eli took Jules by the hand and led her out of Dunleavy's. Denny Griffin was standing at the bar and watched Eli and Jules leave the pub hand in hand. The air outside was hot and thick, and Jules's heart was racing. What she didn't know was that Eli's was too.

"What would you like to do now?" Eli asked.

"I'd like some ice cream and to get out of downtown," Jules said.

"You know I live downtown, right?" Eli looked at her. "Well, a couple of neighborhoods over. I have a townhouse close to the water."

"I didn't know you lived by the water," Jules said, trying to change the subject.

"And I don't know why you don't like being downtown."

"You're not going to let this go, are you?"

Eli shook his head. "Nope."

Jules sighed. "Okay, well, this isn't the kind of thing you can't just 'unknow' once I tell you. And it'll change what you know about me, and I'm not sure if I can handle that."

"Jules, whatever it is, you can tell me."

"I'll tell you when we get to your place by the water… after you get me what just turned into a large ice cream with a few toppings."

Chapter 6

*J*ules held both large cups of ice cream while Eli unlocked and opened the front door to his apartment. The door opened up to the living room, where Eli did all of his entertaining, and the kitchen was behind it. The kitchen had a neat, sort of vintage component: a dumbwaiter, because the spacious townhouse had three floors. The second floor had two bedrooms each, with their own bathrooms, connected by another small living area, which Eli rarely used. The third floor had three rooms and another full bathroom.

They went up to the second-floor den and sat down on the loveseat. Eli had gotten a three-scoop sundae, complete with strawberry, chocolate, and vanilla ice cream; nuts; chocolate-fudge sauce; and cherries. Jules got two scoops: cake batter and caramel-praline swirl, with white chocolate chips and crushed Heath bar pieces.

"You want some of my sundae?" Eli asked Jules.

"No, thanks. I don't like chocolate-fudge sauce or cherries."

"You're kidding. I didn't know that."

"I like chocolate, just not chocolate sauce. I like caramel better, and I hate maraschino cherries but love real cherries. But you can have some of mine if you like."

"What I'd like is to know why you're scared that something you tell me is going to change how I feel about you," Eli said, taking a spoonful of Jules's ice cream.

She exhaled and licked her spoon clean. To begin with, she didn't know how he felt about her. Several times throughout the years, she had given an account of what had happened to her that night, or at least what she could remember and what she'd been told. Now it was Eli who was asking, and a baseball-size lump in her throat was preventing the words from emerging. Jules exhaled again and put her ice cream cup on the coffee table.

"I have something better in mind than talking," she said, as she threw her leg over Eli's lap and straddled him. "Talking is overrated." She positioned herself over his hardening erection. "All you've ever done my entire life is talk to me," she said, planting light kisses on his lips as his hands ran up her back under her shirt.

"Not true," he countered. "I kissed you this morning."

"Yes, you did kiss me this morning." Her light kisses slowly moved up and down his neck, making his craving for her stronger. "But the fact will always remain for the rest of history that I kissed you first." She knew the competitor in him wouldn't let this go.

She laid her lips on top of his, and the moment he'd been dreaming of since he was seventeen presented itself. He was now less concerned with their previous conversation and more concerned with helping Jules shed the barrier that was preventing their skin-to-skin contact. She hadn't planned on having sex with Eli tonight, but the thought of having to tell him what had happened made her want to have him just once before he knew, because once he knew, there was no unknowing.

Eli put his hands under Jules's ass and lifted her as he stood up and walked the twenty feet to his bedroom. He sat her down on his bed and pulled his shirt over his head, and she pulled off hers as well. He crawled onto the bed and straddled her, this time pressing his body into hers and feeling her soft, smooth, milky skin beneath his hands. Her hands traced the muscles of his back; his lats and traps were chiseled, along with his triceps.

Their kissing was rhythmic, almost automatic. Eli couldn't believe he'd been waiting for this more than half his life, and here Jules was—his for the taking. Although she didn't know it yet, he wasn't going to let her go. His strong hands explored her perky, supple breasts, pinching then rubbing. To his surprise, he'd soon find out her breasts were each a perfect mouthful—exactly what he liked.

Right now Eli couldn't tear his lips away from hers to kiss any other parts of her body, and he felt as if he were kissing for each time he had wanted to kiss her when they were younger. Although he'd endured more than ten years of pent-up longing, Jules had no idea about it at all. She figured he might be interested now, because she was kissing him, but it was never anything she would have contemplated before this moment.

Eli's enormous erection was pressing into her stomach. He took his lips from hers and kissed her all the way down from her neck to her belly button, paying special attention to her hardened nipples and the more ticklish areas. Eli unbuttoned her jeans and pulled them off then stood up to remove his pants. For the first time in a long time, he felt nervous and didn't want this to end. Jules seemed to miss his presence for the few seconds that he wasn't touching her. She almost couldn't believe this was actually happening and needed him to touch her to validate that this was real.

Without saying a word, Eli lay back down beside Jules. He was trying to calm himself down to slow the experience. His fingertips lightly grazed her cheeks then her chin before he gently gripped the back of her neck. He looked at her with an intensity she could feel. His intense look made her insides shake, and she wanted to squirm. Eli pulled her to him slightly, and their lips met; they kissed while looking each other in the eyes. Their tongues toyed and tangled with pleasure. Jules tasted sweet to Eli—a little sweet from her ice cream—while her luscious lips were smooth and tart from the pomegranate oil in her lip balm.

The possibility of what might happen in a few minutes screamed across the surface of Jules's skin, making her tear her lips away from those beautiful full lips she used to dream about, and the only word she could articulate was, "Condom." And it was definitely more of a command.

"Oh, no, Miss Bossy. You don't get to control this. I'm enjoying myself right where I am," Eli said, then kissed his way to her aching bud. Jules wanted him so much it physically hurt. She had felt an unsatisfied throbbing between her legs since the day Eli had walked into her dad's office with those contracts. And she couldn't discount the years between the age of twelve and now, during which she secretly had been in love with Eli— but the ache had never been this bad, maybe because she'd never been anywhere near having sex with Eli. Their lips never had even touched before Jules had kissed him on the porch steps last night.

His relentless assault on her clit ceased as soon as she screamed his name. "Eeee-llliiiii! Oh, God, Eli."

He knew Jules was coming as she arched her back and giggled. "What was that?" he asked. "You're not laughing at me, are you?"

"No…my body is tingling," Jules said, propping herself up on her elbow and looking at him.

With his left hand, Eli wiped the moisture from his face then brought his taut body down on top of hers and kissed her. He wanted her to taste her own essence. Eli was absolutely enthralled with Jules, and this experience brought his feelings to a whole new level. He took his lips away from hers, reached over to his left to the nightstand, and grabbed a condom from the drawer. He put the package between his teeth, tore it open, and eagerly slid it onto his penis. These coordinated movements happened in mere seconds. Eli loved to describe himself as a "grown-ass man" when he was playing around, but he was nearly giddy at the thought of making love to Jules and actually thankful for the condom for once. He didn't want to come too quickly; he was intent on devouring her.

Jules was all but begging him, and he knew it. He slid his fingers inside her just to tease her a little more. He wanted to learn Jules's body; he already had learned that she giggled when she came—or at least she did when he made her come—and he adored that smile…and that sound. He wanted to *make* her make that little giggle; in fact he would delight in it.

He broke his lips away in a gasp, as his lungs and brain both required air. Jules's tongue made contact with Eli's neck. She kissed and nipped her way up to his earlobe, and then it was Eli who couldn't wait any longer.

Without a word, Eli placed the head of his cock at the moist entrance to her wanting pussy. He didn't hesitate, but he moved in slowly. Jules moaned into his mouth as his rock-hard cock pressed farther into her tight channel, and then he hit *that* spot. From her reaction, he knew it and did all he could to stimulate that spot.

"Uhh, oohh. Ahh, ahh. Oh, babe…oh, oh, oh…*oui, bébe, oui*…oh, yes." Jules exhaled, and then she giggled as her walls tightened around his magnificent cock.

"That might be the nicest thing you've ever said to me, babe," Eli teased, as he grabbed the outside of her thighs with his giant hands to pull her closer to him. She wrapped her legs a little higher than his waist; the emotion was love, but the action was fucking. And it was fucking amazing…*He was fucking amazing.* He couldn't keep his hands or lips—or tongue for that matter—off her. They might have known each other forever, but this was entirely new territory.

Jules tried to roll over on top of Eli, but she was no match for him. He was almost a whole foot taller than her, and she had nowhere near his strength. He pinned her and looked her in the eyes then said, "Don't move."

Eli grabbed a small pillow and put it under her luscious ass. He interlaced his fingers with hers and placed her hands above her head. Then he lowered his lips to hers and kissed her sweetly (as he planned to every day from here on out) while he fucked her pussy as though it was what he'd been practicing for. About five to seven minutes later and two or three orgasms for Jules, Eli finally came. Neither of them spoke for what seemed minutes. He exhaled a few times then kissed his way up her neck to her lips.

"Hi," he said, looking into her eyes.

"Hi," she replied. "I think we might have ruined your pillow."

"Are you kidding?" Eli said, taking it out from beneath her. "This just became my favorite pillow." He put the pillow under his head then added, "I enjoyed that immensely; you have no way of knowing just how much I *enjoyed* that, and this next statement is solely for my own amusement."

"Uh-huh" was all she could muster.

"I just made love...to my best friend's baby sister."

"'Made love,' huh? Shouldn't it be 'banged,' 'fucked,' 'screwed,' 'shagged,' or something?"

"'Penetrated,'" he shot back.

"Oh, my God, Chris would hate that so much. Please tell him and use that word," she exclaimed, and he laughed. "I always hate it when sports commentators use the word 'penetrate.'"

"Jules," Eli said, lying on his side and looking at her through heavy-lidded eyes, "this is the most unlikely conversation...and that was the most amazing sex of my life, and I was wearing a damn condom."

"Aww...I bet you say that to all the girls," she said slyly.

"For the record, Ms. Dempsey, I've never uttered such words. If I'd said it before, it would have been a lie. I know I'm a lawyer, but I'm more of a 'legal stylist' than a liar per se. And please...no more 'man-whore' jokes," he said without a smile. "Let's just say I've required lots of distractions to take my mind off what I couldn't have," Eli confessed.

Without questioning his statement, Jules got up, picked up the tank top Eli had worn under his shirt, and put it on while making her way toward the bathroom.

"You're not leaving me now, are you?" Eli asked.

"No, silly. I have to pee. I'll be right back. Plus, you drove me here—where am I going?"

Eli pinched himself a few times to make sure he was awake and this was really happening. Then he high-fived himself. After cleaning herself up and peeing, Jules crawled back into bed. Neither of them tried to make small talk; they both just fell asleep. Eli was spooning Jules, who was sure she was going to wake up alone and this was going to be the most phenomenal erotic dream of her life.

Jules's eyes opened about twenty minutes to eight on Saturday morning. She was in a completely different position than where she had started out the night before. Eli's arms were wrapped around her, while she was on her side, with an arm across his body, and their legs were in a tangled mess. When Jules awoke, Eli had his head propped up on his "favorite pillow" and was watching the news on MSNBC.

"Hi, Sleeping Beauty. Good morning," Eli chirped.

"'Morning. How long have you been up?" Jules asked.

Eli shrugged. "Since a little after seven, I think. I try not to pay attention to the time on the weekends."

"Would you be willing to take me home once I fully wake up?"

"Sure, but do you want some breakfast? Maybe you'd like to take a shower?"

"No...I'm good, and I don't have any clean clothes to change into if I took a shower," Jules said, as she got up to collect her clothing and get dressed. She took off Eli's tank top so she could put her bra and shirt on, and he picked it up and put it on over his marvelous chest.

As Jules pulled on her jeans, Eli hated the thought of her leaving. He stood up and closed the space between them. Then he put both hands on each side of her face and tilted her head up slightly. "I'm not ready to take you home yet," he said before he placed his lips over hers.

She returned the kiss then pulled away. "If you start this now, I'll miss my eleven a.m. curfew."

"Can I see you again tonight?" Eli asked.

"I'm not sure what's going on at home, but if there's nothing pressing, I don't see why not," Jules said, as she smoothed her shirt over her torso and pulled her hair up into a ponytail.

"C'mon, Jules, there is *something pressing,*" Eli said.

"I wouldn't want you thinking I'm that easy, just because I kind of slept with you on the first date."

"*Second.* It was our second date. And I'm not complaining," he said, as he watched her put on her sneakers.

"It was the first time I came to your house, and I'm not complaining either…it's just…"

"It's just what, Jules?"

"I don't want things to be weird between us," she said pointedly.

"Weird how? Nothing's going to be weird. We've known each other for a long time, and last night it didn't seem that either of us needed any convincing. You weren't worried about it being weird when you straddled me to distract me from our conversation in the den."

"I was being spontaneous. And I thought it'd be more fun than talking," she argued.

"You're not telling me something," he said, stating the obvious, "and you used your gorgeous body to distract me."

"Well, it worked, didn't it?

"Yes, it did," he admitted.

That's because I wanted to have you one time before you run away from me screaming in horror. Jules smiled at Eli. "Can we keep last night just between us?"

Eli grinned back. "Well, I was going to take out a front-page ad, but since you asked me not to, I guess I'll keep it to myself. And since you're already dressed and don't want a shower or breakfast," he said, as they walked out the front door to the car, "I guess I'll take you home now."

During the ride back to the Dempsey's home, Eli held Jules's hand close to his face and placed light kisses on her palm and fingers. She was trying to calm the panic that was vibrating through her body. Eli looked so sweet in the morning sunlight, holding her hand next to his lips. Jules was actually relieved when he pulled up to the curb in front of her house.

"How about if I make dinner for you tonight?" Eli asked.

"That depends on your cooking skills," Jules responded.

"I can throw down, but if you want, we can make dinner together," Eli proposed.

"On one condition."

"Name it."

"Don't walk me to the door. My ma and grandma aren't going to let this go—the fact that I spent the night with you. If you walk me to the door, it'll just intensify the situation. So please say good-bye to me right here, especially if you want to see me later."

"Okay, okay. I guess I'll just have to get my kisses now." He leaned over the center console and planted his lips over hers. "Since I'm not walking you to the door, I want you back at my place tonight," he urged.

"I'll text you when I'm on my way," she said.

"And I'll text you with dinner options."

Jules kept her body in the open space, facing Eli, and put her fingertips underneath his chin. "You have to have a little patience," she said before she lightly kissed his lips.

"It's hard to have patience when you know what you want." His eyes met hers, and he gave her a quick peck on the lips then suggested she go or he might not be able to stop himself.

The walk from Eli's Land Rover to the front door was tantamount to an odyssey. So many things had happened between last night when she had walked out the front door and her return this morning. Besides the fact that she and Eli had been intimate, he'd made it explicitly clear he wanted to see her again. Jules's body shook with excitement, nerves, and bewilderment.

Chapter 7

*I*t was just past 9:00 a.m. when Jules walked into her parents' house.

"Hello?" she called out, loudly enough for anyone downstairs to hear her.

"In here," she heard from the kitchen.

Helene and Lovey were sitting at the kitchen counter, having coffee. The two of them looked like they were going to explode with excitement. They both seemed to be staring intently at her.

"Good morning," Jules said before kissing both of them on the cheek, and they responded in kind. "Where are you and Martha having lunch today, Lovey?"

"The Langham, dear. It's the only place where she'll eat anymore."

"There's a spa there, right?" Jules asked.

"I believe so. Why?"

"I think while you and Martha are visiting, I'll get a pedicure and a massage."

"Well, it must be true," Lovey stated.

"What's that?" asked Jules.

"Obviously friends do make the *best* lovers...since you need a massage and all."

"Lovey!"

"Don't be embarrassed, *ma petite.* I've been waiting for the two of you to get together since Eli was in eleventh grade," Helene said, sounding a bit exasperated.

"Eleventh grade? Ma, have you been drinking Irish coffee this morning? Eleventh grade! You're crazy. Eli was dating a pageant queen then."

"*Ma petite bijou,* it doesn't matter who he was dating. A mother knows, and that boy has been sweet on you for a long time."

"*Maman!*"

Lovey smiled. "Spill it, girlie."

"There's nothing to spill. You both act like I was going to come back engaged to Eli."

"*Hoping* is more like it," Helene said.

"We went to the bar, and I met some of his friends and watched the game. Eli mentioned that he had bought a few new movies that neither of us had seen, so we got some ice cream, and then we fell asleep on the couch."

"You're not telling us everything," Lovey said, as Jules was stuffing her face with the fresh fruit Helene was cutting at the kitchen counter.

"You're right, Lovey. I'm not telling you everything," Jules said with a sly smile.

Lovey and Helene looked at each other with anticipation.

"We're going to make dinner together tonight. If anything interesting happens, I'll make sure you two beg for it," Jules said laughingly as she headed upstairs to take a shower.

"She has it bad for him," Lovey said, grinning, "and she deserves something good."

Panic and disbelief had settled over Jules, and it was all she could do to remind herself to breathe. Eli's sandalwood scent enveloped her; every time she inhaled, all she could smell was him. When she walked into her bedroom, she picked up the vaporizer and plugged it into an outlet in the bathroom. She lit the candle under the lavender-oil diffuser and turned on the shower.

Holy fucking shit! Holy. Fucking. Shit. I can't believe we did that. Holy fucking shit. I had sex with Eli. "Made love"…those were his words. Holy fucking shit. Oh, God, what have I done? It must not have been too bad, because he wants to see me again tonight. He wants us to make dinner…together.

The hot water felt wonderful on her exhilarated body. Jules was almost giddy, but she also was terrified. What if all Eli wanted was sex? To be fair, she did start it because she didn't want to explain her fears to him, but how was she going to stop it if that was all he wanted? Her phone rang, and she hoped it was Eli, but she was relieved when it wasn't. Still in the shower, she grabbed the phone from the counter next to the sink and poked her head out.

"Nettie, can I call you back in a minute?" she said. "I'm in the shower."

"No, sweetie. I'm getting on a plane to Chicago," Annette said. "Call Lorraine, my realtor. She has a few additional properties for you to look at. I'll text you her number in a few minutes, once I get situated in my seat."

"Thanks, Nettie. Safe travels."

Annette hung up, and Jules turned around to rinse her hair. She still had to take Lovey to lunch with Martha. Every Saturday for years, Martha had lunch at the Langham. Standing there in the shower, Jules decided she was going to get as many spa services as she could fit in during Lovey's lunch with Martha. As soon as she got out of the shower, she called and booked a Brazilian wax, a facial, a pedicure, and a massage. Then she called Lorraine.

"Lorraine Anderson speaking," Lorraine pleasantly chirped.

"Hi, Lorraine. This is Jules Dempsey. I'm a friend of—"

"Annette's," she interrupted. "I remember you well. I spoke with her a few days ago. She told me you were closer to purchasing a property."

"I am, and I'd like to be within twenty blocks of the office, give or take a few, but I don't really want to live on the East Side either."

"Give me a range for location, style, and price."

"Between the twenties to the sixties. Apartment or brownstone is preferable, no studios, and I don't want my mortgage to be more than five thousand to seven thousand a month. I don't want to be house poor. Access to a garage might be necessary."

"That sounds reasonable," Lorraine said. "Do you have a move-in date in mind?"

"No, right now I'm taking care of my grandmother in Boston, so I'm not looking to move in anytime soon, but if we come across a property that's too good to pass up, then it'll be waiting for me. My grandmother wants me to find something she approves of before she passes because she wants to gift me the down payment."

"That's a generous gift, and thanks for letting me know that ahead of time. I'll get back to you in a few days. Do you think you could arrange to come to New York this coming Thursday and Friday so we could look at properties?"

"Maybe, but I don't know right this second," Jules said.

"All right, I know there are quite a few properties you'd be interested in within the parameters you gave me. I just need to put my hands on my computer, and then I'll e-mail them to you. You decide on the ones you want to see, let me know, and I'll schedule the viewings whenever you can be here. Text me your e-mail address, please."

"Absolutely. Thanks so much, Lorraine."

"No problem. Talk to you soon."

Jules hung up and pulled on some gray yoga pants and a purple tank top with a built-in bra. She saw absolutely no reason to do her hair or makeup, so she just brushed her teeth and then her hair, and then she went downstairs. Lovey was sitting on the couch, working on a blanket she was knitting.

"Lovey, you want to come upstairs and make sure you're good and hungry for lunch?"

Lovey's eyes lit up. "You know I do. What time is it?"

"It's almost eleven, so we probably have thirty minutes to kill. My first service isn't until noon."

Mary Dempsey and her only granddaughter went up to Jules's room to log some more time with the vaporizer. Jules got ridiculously stoned because she realized she was going to have to tell Eli some extremely sensitive information tonight.

"Spill it, girlie. I want to know all the details about your night out with Eli," Lovey encouraged.

"I told you. We watched a movie, and I must've fallen asleep first." Jules inhaled from the vaporizer and let out a long exhale.

"Did he at least kiss you?"

"He came to the pool and kissed me Friday morning after our date Thursday night."

Lovey's eyes got big as she inhaled. "You didn't tell me that!"

"I wasn't trying to get anyone's hopes up." *Least of all my own.*

"And he wants to see you again tonight? He sure didn't waste any time."

"I was surprised he wanted to have dinner again tonight."

"You shouldn't be surprised. He's more interested than you think, and I think there's more happening than you're telling me."

Jules looked away, exhaled, then hit the vaporizer again. "I realized yesterday that if he and I are going to have any type of relationship where feelings are involved, I have to tell him what happened when I was a teenager."

"You listen to me, young lady—if he feels about you the way I think he does, he's not going to care. That won't stop him."

"Yeah, but I care."

"I know you do, honey," Lovey said, patting her hand.

When they were finished, Jules drove her grandmother to the Langham, a large hotel downtown, to visit with one of her oldest friends. The smooth stone exterior housed a classic yet modern interior. Its shiny marble floors led patrons into to the large welcoming area, over which three incredible chandeliers were suspended. Each was made up of two hundred or more glass wreaths comprised of glass balls, while a large, hollow, circular tube ran through the middle of the wreaths.

Jules really wanted the two hours during the facial and massage to think—or *not* think, if necessary. Actually it was two hours during which she wouldn't have to be tied to her phone, since she'd have to turn it off. Lovey and Martha would be all set at the expensive restaurant, and Jules informed the maître d' that she would be in the spa if she were needed for any reason.

Jules made her way to the elevator. When she arrived at the spa, she was given a robe and asked to undress and sit in the quiet, calming, dimly lit waiting area. Eucalyptus and lavender wafted through the air, furthering the calm settling over her.

The spa had some Asian undertones; from the sporadically placed bonsai trees, to the constant sound of flowing water, this little oasis breathed serenity. Throughout the spa, the sound of stone chimes floated in the air.

Jules wanted to relax; she *needed* to relax. The Brazilian wax came first. The table was comfortable; Jules lay down and closed her eyes. The moment she did, she felt Eli's tongue sliding down her body. Every single moment from last night came flooding back. The fresh memories didn't relent during the facial, pedicure, or massage. By the end of her spa services, she was more relaxed, but the throbbing between her legs had returned. This return "home" wasn't at all going how she had expected.

While Lovey and Martha were saying their good-byes, another woman they knew walked up and began to chat with them. Jules sighed and reminded herself to be patient. As she sat waiting for Lovey, her phone sounded.

How does stuffed shells sound? Eli asked.

We just had Italian, Jules responded.

E: *True. What do you want?*

J: *What do you have?*

E: *Pork chops, steak, salmon, and nacho fixings.*

J: *Steak sounds good. Do you have potatoes and stuff to make a salad with?*

E: *If that's what you want.*

J: *You cook the steak—I like mine medium. And I'll make the baked potatoes and salad.*

E: *When are you coming?*

J: *In a little while.*

E: *Time?*

J: *It's about half past two right now.*

E: *Jules, what time are you coming to me?*

J: *Probably around six.*

E: *Not soon enough.*

J: *Five?*

E: *Better—not much, but better. See you soon*

❦

At 5:15 a knock came at Eli's door. Jules was so nervous she was sure he would see her shaking. He opened the door wearing a broad smile.

"I thought you were coming over at five," he said, as he welcomed her in and shut the door behind her.

Jules spun on her heels to respond to Eli's statement. Before she could get a word out, he put his hands on her waist and kissed her as though he hadn't seen her in days. She wrapped her arms around his neck, and he leaned her back a little.

"What was that for?" she asked, as she slowly opened her eyes. If it weren't for Eli's hands around her waist, she would have lost her balance and fallen over.

"You made me wait too long to see you, and I couldn't help myself." He took her by the hand and led her to the kitchen, where he was heating up the grill top.

"Wait too long for what? It's barely after five, and I'm here," Jules said.

"You said you would be here at five, and you weren't."

"Did you turn on the oven for the baked potatoes, or were you too busy counting the minutes of my tardiness?" Jules asked, leaning against the counter while thumbing through a copy of *TIME* magazine.

"I did, but it takes almost an hour to thoroughly bake potatoes," Eli said, as he pressed the front of his body into the back of Jules's and wrapped his arms around her, "so I preheated the oven and put the potatoes in already."

"Then all I have to do is make the salad?" Jules questioned.

"Well, it turned out that I didn't have anything to make a salad with, so I called McCarthy's and ordered two large salads to go. They're in the fridge," Eli admitted.

"Then what do you want me to do? I don't know how to cook steak." She smiled as she turned around to face him.

"Just continue being beautiful and enjoy the dinner I made for you," he said, leaning in to kiss her.

"Oh, no! You can't take all the credit. McCarthy's helped," Jules quipped as she hoisted herself up to sit on the counter.

Eli positioned himself between her knees, against the counter, and simply couldn't help himself. He slid her close to him. They were almost eye to eye, and Eli couldn't have stopped if he tried—and of course he didn't want to.

Jules was breathless when she tore her lips away and tilted her head down to get some air. She inhaled deeply then exhaled as she put her forehead down on his chest.

"What is it?" Eli asked with a light chuckle.

"First, I don't think I'm hungry right now. And second, I've never been kissed the way you kiss me."

"Is that a bad thing?" he asked, adjusting the temperature of the grill top to the lowest setting.

"No, it's not a bad thing at all. It's just that…not even the man who was in love with me kissed me like that," she almost whispered.

"Maybe he wasn't really in love with you." He returned to the counter where she was sitting. "Tell me about this man who was in love with you. The one who didn't kiss you right."

"Hold on now…I didn't say he didn't kiss me right. I said he didn't kiss me the way you do," Jules retorted.

"Means the same thing to me," came Eli's cocky response. "So tell me about him."

"No, it's rude. I didn't come here to talk about him."

"Wait…you're not still with him, are you?" Eli asked pensively.

"Eli, think about that question and how ridiculous it is. I slept with you less than twenty-four hours ago. And neither of us seems to be able to keep our lips or hands off each other. None of that would have happened if I were still with him. So do you want to retract your question?" She cut her eyes at him while he was smiling that cocky smile as he opened the fridge to get some water.

Eli laughed. "Good, because I want you all to myself…and I want you tell me about this guy who was in love with you."

"What does it matter? I'm sure right now Javi is surrounded by exotic women, somewhere warm—a place that doesn't extradite to the US."

"Why would he need to be extradited? And what kind of name is Javi?"

"It's short for Javier, and I have no knowledge of his past or present dealings…or knowledge of where he is, but I know where he's not. He's not in Miami, or Boston for that matter."

"How long were you with him?" Eli probed.

"Four years…ish. And are you willing to answer these same questions about all the women you've been with, counselor? I feel like I'm being interrogated."

"Don't change the subject. I'll answer any questions you have."

"I'm calling bullshit—you can't seriously remember all the women you've been with in the last eight years or so."

"You might have a point, but you said 'been with' not 'been in love with.'"

"Were you in love with any of them?" Jules wondered aloud.

"I loved a few of them, but it wasn't like that first love," he admitted.

"Is it ever? Is it ever really like the first love?" She looked at him intently.

"Was Chavi your first love?"

"I don't know anyone named Chavi, but if you're referring to *Javi,* no, he wasn't my first love. It was more like he brought me back from the edge. So really you should be thanking him. It's because of him that I'm sitting here right now."

Eli gave her a confused look. "What are you talking about?"

"It's okay…I really don't want to talk about it, or Javi, right now. I came over to see you. You're the only person I've spent any social time with since I've been here, and coincidentally you're just about the only person I want to be around. Don't let all this go to your head now, but you make me feel safe, and you're certainly the bright spot in my day. So make me my damn dinner and shut up about all this other shit, aiight? Please, Eli." Jules was stressed, and Eli could see it; that wasn't what he wanted.

"Okay, no more talk about the guy who wasn't your first love…So who was?"

"Who was what?" she asked, still looking through the magazine.

"Who was your first love?"

Jules didn't answer.

"I'll tell you, if you tell me," Eli prodded in a singsong voice.

"E-ee-lllii," she whined.

"Man, you don't want to talk about any of this," Eli said.

Jules glared at him. He knew that look, so he found a bottle of wine to open.

"Do you want red or white?"

"Red…I don't like white. It gives me a headache; it has more chemicals than red does. Roberto taught me how to drink wine like a professional."

"Can I ask who Roberto is?" Eli said.

"He's Javi's uncle. He's a sommelier at one of the three-star restaurants he and the chef co-own. I was a hostess for a little while, and then I started doing the books. During that time, I ate exquisite food and drank the most luscious wines."

"Oh, yeah? What's your favorite type of red?"

"I love a good shiraz or cabernet," Jules said. "There are some amazing pinot noirs too. I like to drink merlot if it's paired with dinner, but I think it's too heavy just for drinking…at least for my taste."

"I have a cab-merlot mix. Is that okay?"

"That works," Jules said, smiling.

That little change of subject, to Jules's favorite wines, kept her talking about that for a little while. The wine they were drinking tasted of cherries, chocolate, currant, and plum. It was delicious. She relayed stories of absolutely delectable food, while Eli entertained her by describing the various types of ethnic foods he had eaten while in the Peace Corps. To Jules he sounded as though he were narrating episodes of *Bizarre Foods with Andrew Zimmern,* but she liked listening to him talk. They had spent so much time apart, each thinking fondly of each other. Time had changed them and made them the people they were supposed to be right at this moment.

It was nearly six, and Jules was starting to get hungry. As she finished the last sip of wine in her glass, Eli rounded the bar, checking on the potatoes.

"Are they done?" Jules asked.

"No, they need a few minutes. I figured I'd start something I could finish in the next fifteen minutes," Eli said, wiggling his eyebrows.

"What about the steaks?"

"The steaks won't take that long to cook, and we can eat the salad while they're on the grill. So if you have no further questions, I'm going to take you to the couch and make love to you. I missed you all day," he said, as he lifted her up and hoisted her over his shoulder caveman style.

Eli nearly ran the few yards from the kitchen to the couch and climbed onto it with both knees before lowering Jules down the front of his body. When her knees hit the couch, she wrapped her arms around his neck. They kissed as he pressed her into his body.

"Jules—" he started.

"Shh!" she snapped as she stood up, pulled her spaghetti straps down, and shimmied out of her tank top and yoga pants in one smooth motion. Eli was staring at her perky boobs. With both arms encircling her waist, he licked, kissed, tickled, and nibbled any exposed skin he could touch. As Jules lowered her head to kiss him, he lowered her body to the couch underneath him. Their lips met, and Eli looked into Jules's eyes.

"All the condoms are upstairs, babe," he warned.

"I don't have anything contagious, but are you too lazy to go upstairs?" she said with a smirk.

"Good, neither do I, and I'm not lazy—I'm just not letting you go," he said before he kissed her again. All those years ago, he never thought he'd be making love to his dream girl. "Jules, wrap your legs around my hips," he said. She did, and he picked her up and sat down on the couch, putting her in the dominant position, just as she'd been when she had thrown her leg over him and kissed him the first time they'd had sex.

Jules wasn't sure she was going to be able to be in control like this—his junk was huge. She already was wet as she sat up on her knees and leaned toward him.

"Be easy there, King Kong," she whispered.

"The last thing I want is to hurt you." He exhaled deeply as Jules grabbed his dick with her left hand and got off him.

Before he could protest, the tip of his dick was in her mouth, and to Eli it was the most incredible feeling in the world. Her plump, pouty lips worked the head of his cock like it was a Blow Pop.

His head fell backward to the couch as her tongue swirled around his cock. Eli thought both his "heads" were going to explode. "Oh, God, Jules…please…please don't stop." Jules took his delicious dick in her mouth as far as she could, but that wasn't far. Barely half of it was covered, and that magnificent piece of equipment he was working with hit the back of her throat. She used her hands to rub from the base to where her mouth met his cock.

"Wait, wait, stop!" Eli exclaimed as he sat forward and gripped her shoulders.

Jules looked up at him and licked her lips. "What's wrong?"

"I…I…you're gonna make me come," he said, exasperated.

She smiled. "That's sort of the point."

"Not before you," he said, leading her to his lap then licking his left hand and touching her wet spot.

Jules smiled into Eli's kiss while she positioned herself over his fully erect cock and slid down just over the head. She slowly worked her way down and let her tight channel adjust to the position. All at once, it seemed as though he were poking the bottom of her internal organs—she just sat there and looked at him. He ran both hands up the sides of her body to her face, fisted her hair, and tilted her head back slightly. Kisses with alternating lips and tongue rained down her neck as she slowly moved up and down on his thick cock. Maybe two minutes later, as Eli felt her channel tighten and spasm, she went limp into his embrace as millions of little explosions erupted all over her body. It wasn't Jules's first orgasm, but it was by far the most intense sensation she'd ever experienced. Then she started giggling. Eli breathed a sigh of relief because he'd been about to bust since Jules had put his dick in her mouth.

In one motion, he picked Jules up under her arms and off his penis just before he came. He hadn't thought this part through very thoroughly. Possibly, the worst thing that would happen if he hadn't pulled out in time was that he would get her pregnant, which wouldn't be so bad. He actually didn't mind that thought at all. That was a very selfish thing to think, considering he wasn't sure what her plans were.

Their sweaty bodies were sticking to each other as Eli smiled into Jules's neck. They were both breathing as though they'd just finished a marathon. Hard breaths were pushed out of—then pulled into—gasping lungs. It hadn't even been a whole ten minutes, but they were exhausted.

"If I wasn't hungry before, I am now," Jules said through heavy eyelids.

"Well, it's a good thing the potatoes are finished and the steaks only take about fifteen minutes," Eli said, as he stood both of their bodies upright. He handed her the T-shirt he'd been wearing, and he pulled on his boxer briefs. Then he reached down, kissed her, and led her into the kitchen so he could grill the steaks.

Fifteen minutes later, they sat down to dinner together, with her wearing only his shirt and him wearing his briefs. Less than thirty minutes later, all of Jules's salad was gone, and she had eaten about half her baked potato and more than half of her eight-ounce steak.

Eli replenished her wine. "Do you want me to open another bottle?" he asked, as he cleared the table and put the dishes in the sink.

"Oh, no, I have to drive home, remember? Unless you want to represent me for a DUI," Jules said with a laugh.

"You aren't going anywhere, Ms. Dempsey." Eli closed the space between them, put his gigantic hands on either side of her face, and kissed her. "Did you enjoy your dinner?" he asked, stroking the sides of her face with his thumbs.

"I did. Thank you. My steak was cooked perfectly—medium, good texture, tender. The salad was good too. Did you marinate the steak?"

"Yeah, in fruit juice."

"Really? What kind?"

"I took an apple, orange, pineapple, mango, and a papaya and juiced them then soaked the fillets all day," Eli said, spilling his secret. "There was a man in Peru, Rey Diaz, who built the school where I taught English. He taught me how to marinate and grill steak."

"He taught you well, and you were a fabulous student, because that steak was perfect. And the potato was steaming hot when I cut into it. Is there anything you can't do, Eli?"

Eli just stood there and looked at her. *I can't stop thinking about you—that's what I can't do,* he thought. He came out of his daydream still staring at her while she was saying, "Earth to Eli."

"Thanks for the *dessert* before dinner," she said with a shy smile, "and thanks for making me dinner. It was delicious."

"But…" he interjected.

"I need to get dressed and go."

"It's barely nine," he nearly whined.

"I know, but I have a long day tomorrow with Lovey, and it starts early. Instead of going to church, she's going to work out and then have brunch with some ladies. Trust me, I'd much rather do that than go to church. Monday morning she has two doctor's appointments, then a workout, followed by lunch with some ladies from the physical rehab clinic."

He wanted to ask her what she was doing Sunday afternoon, but he thought better of it because she seemed to be on the fringe of a freak-out. Eli moved to where she was, embraced her, and rested his head on top of hers. "Will you come by the office Monday?"

"At some point I'm sure I will, but I can't give you a definite time right this minute."

"Maybe you'll text me when you're on the way, so if I'm not there, I can get back. You know I want you stay with me tonight, right?" Eli asked, using his best puppy-dog eyes.

Jules smiled. "You've said that once or twice. Are you trying to guilt me into staying?"

"Sort of…Is it working?"

"Eli, there isn't much I wouldn't do for you, so don't make that sad face at me. You have no idea how exhausting my grandmother can be. I need to be well rested for her tomorrow and Monday."

"Well, after you change back into your clothes, I'll walk you out to your car," he said, sounding a bit macho and protective.

It was nearly ten by the time Eli was walking Jules to her car. Jules promised to text him as soon as she got home. She held true to her word and texted him when she pulled into the driveway and then again when she got into bed. She had no idea what was happening in her relationship with Eli, but it scared the absolute shit out of her. This turn of events, in her mind, hadn't even been in the realm of possibility of things that could happen when she had come back to Boston. Eli never had factored anywhere into the equation. The whole situation was too much for her emotionally, she thought, as she drifted off to sleep.

Chapter 8

Wednesday evening

Jules had barely spoken to or seen Eli in four days. He was short-tempered and irritated because she seemed to have made herself scarce in the last few days. Was she avoiding him? Did he do something wrong? Eli didn't know, but he was going to find out.

It was a little after seven, and Helene's book club was in deep conversation about a novel set in sixteenth-century England titled *And They All Fall Down*. Lovey looked forward to book club; she enjoyed Helene's friends and their varying perspectives. Mostly she liked the fact that all the ladies enjoyed a glass of wine or two…or three. When wine entered the mix, their tongues loosened some, and then the conversations became really interesting.

Eli rang the doorbell. Jules was in the kitchen, washing dishes; she dried her hands and headed for the door. Her heart dropped when she opened it to see Eli standing there. Before she could say anything, he reached out and snatched her up into a deep kiss. Jules was caught off guard and struggled to get away from him. The look on his face expressed confusion and hurt.

"Eli!" she hush-screamed, as she grabbed him by the hand and led him into the sitting room to the left of the front door. "What are you doing? You can't just come to my parents' house and kiss me at the front door!"

"I had to do something. You've been avoiding me for four days," Eli said, with that hurt and confused look on his face again.

"Oh, Eli, I'm not avoiding you—" she started.

"Yes, you are," he said, looking her directly in the eyes.

"You're right…I am," she admitted.

"Did I do something wrong?"

"No. This is all me."

"C'mon, Jules, don't give me that 'It's me, not you' shit. What's wrong?"

"I can't get into it with you right now, seeing as how my ma has her book club in the next room. Are you too busy to reschedule your day tomorrow and Friday?"

"I don't have any meetings scheduled until Tuesday. What did you have in mind?"

"Whenever I'm finished taking care of Lovey, I have a job waiting for me in New York. Tomorrow morning I'm going to the city to look at a few properties. Lovey is helping me with the down payment and wants me to buy a place there before she eventually passes away. Do you want to keep me company on my road trip?"

"Only if you promise to explain what's going on with you and why you've been avoiding me."

"We're going to be in a car together for four hours with nowhere to go. I'll explain everything. I promise, Eli." She took a step toward him and stood on her tiptoes to reach his lips. He met her halfway and kissed her for a few moments on the lips, and then he kissed her on the forehead. "I'll be at your place at seven a.m.," she said, looking up at him.

"When are we coming back?" Eli asked.

"Sunday morning, and don't worry—I've taken care of the sleeping arrangements. I'll see you in the morning. Now I need to get back in the kitchen." Jules scooted Eli out the door and walked back into the kitchen to find her dad picking at the hors d'oeuvres.

"Hey, Dad. Ma said you can't have any because you didn't read the book."

"Well, if you don't tell her I'm eating her party food, I won't tell her I saw you and Eli kissing in the front room."

Jules smiled at him. "So…are you blackmailing me now? How can you be so sure of what you saw anyway? You don't even have your glasses on."

"It's not blackmail, kid. It's just a little leverage," Thomas said, returning the smirk.

"If it makes you feel any better, Eli is going with me to New York tomorrow."

Thomas raised an eyebrow. "Is he moving there with you?"

"No, Daddy. He's just going to keep me company on the ride."

"Kid, the only way I'd feel better about your living in New York would be if Eli was moving there with you," he said, then kissed his daughter the her cheek, picked up his plate of stolen hors d'oeuvres, and sneaked off to his study until his wife came to find him after the party ended.

A few minutes after seven the next morning, Jules knocked on Eli's front door. Eli answered with a cup in his hand.

"Good morning, sunshine. You ready?" Jules asked, walking inside the townhouse.

"Yep. Hang on—let me grab my bag—and this is for you." He handed her the paper cup then picked up his duffel bag from the floor next to the door.

"Thanks, Eli, and I know this sounds terribly bitchy, but I don't like coffee, remember?"

"I remember…It's not coffee. I made some black tea for you. I let it cool some, added some agave nectar, then poured it over some ice."

Jules grinned. "Wow. 'Thank you' seems inadequate somehow."

"Does it deserve a kiss?" Eli asked hopefully.

"Absolutely," she said, reaching up on her tippy toes. "In fact it deserves so much more than that, but we need to get on the road."

"Well, we do need to go, but every time we get ready to start our conversation, you precede to engage me in earth-shattering sex, and we never seem to get to the conversation part," Eli pointed out, as he locked the door to his townhouse and followed her to the car.

"Earth-shattering, huh?" Jules asked, pleasantly surprised.

"Yep, why?"

"I know I promised to lay off the 'man-whore' jabs, so I'll leave that alone," she said, starting Helene's BMW. Jules sipped on her sweet tea as they merged on to the interstate. She knew she might as well go ahead and get this conversation started so she could get it over with.

"So tell me about this trip to New York," Eli said, giving her a reprieve for the time being.

"Like I said last night, I have a job waiting for me. There was a woman I did some consulting for in Miami—her name is Annette, but I call her 'Nettie.' She owns a midsize company that manages about eighty properties across the globe. I figured out that her finance manager was embezzling money…a lot of money. She fired him, pressed charges, and offered me his job at twice his salary. You and I are going to stay at her place on 81st; she's on a business trip right now. Her place is great, right near Central Park West. Nettie splits her time between Miami and New York, but she doesn't really care for the city and said she needs someone there she trusts, so she offered me the job. Regardless of when I get there, I'll need a place to live." Silence descended upon them for a few minutes as they sipped their drinks.

"Jules, are you—"

"Eli you have to let me do this without interrupting me, or I might not be able to get this out."

Here goes nothing, she thought. "First of all, I've been in love with you since I was twelve, but I couldn't properly identify those feelings until I was about fourteen. I think my realization of this insanity crystallized the first day of school my freshman year. Chris was driving, and we picked you up. I got out to get in the backseat, and you were standing so close to me that I could feel you breathe…and you smelled like Cool Water and baby powder."

Eli was staring at her, smiling. "Johnson's baby powder and Cool Water cologne."

"Lodi dodi, we like to party…Thank you, Snoop Dogg," Jules said with a giggle.

"You know," Eli said, "I started listening to that album because I heard it coming from your room one day, and I wanted to have something to talk to you about."

"It's a great album. While I'm at it, I might as well tell you I stole one of your T-shirts," she said, keeping her eyes focused straight ahead.

"Really? Which one?"

"A brown T-shirt that says BROWN in faded white letters."

Eli laughed. "That was the first T-shirt I bought at Brown. I got it during orientation, and I always wondered what happened to it."

"Well, now you know. I think it was Christmas break during your freshman year at Brown. You and Chris came home, and there was a pickup game of some sort, and you both got dirty. Ma said you boys couldn't come into the house with your dirty clothes on, and she made you strip and said she'd wash your clothes. She did in fact wash your clothes, but she told me to dry and fold them. That's when I took your shirt. When Ma asked me about it, I played dumb and told her I folded what was in the dryer. I slept in it some, but I didn't want to have to keep washing it. After it was washed that first time, it still smelled like you, so I slept with it instead of wearing it. I still have it…and I didn't really plan on telling you all this," Jules said, somewhat embarrassed.

She was quiet for a few moments before she continued. "This thing I have to tell you—this detail you're so interested in knowing—will change everything. The fifteen-year-old inside me has been in total shock ever since you swam up behind me in the pool last week. And I've been pinching myself ever since. You have no idea what you're doing to me.

You are—literally, figuratively, and metaphorically—the only bright spot I've found in Boston."

"Jules, I promise you that whatever it is, it can't possibly change the way I feel about you," Eli said. "And I have a confession of my own."

"Oh, yeah, what's that?"

"I took something of yours too."

"Nah, uh, no way," she said, shaking her head in exaggerated disbelief.

"Ms. Dempsey, let the record show that on one particular afternoon when I showed up at your house to get Chris, he, true to form, was in the shower, which meant I had to wait. Huge surprise! Your mom told me to wait in the family room; she'd been folding laundry and watching one of her DIY shows. When I pushed the ottoman back to put my feet up, I noticed a pair of lavender panties on the floor. I snatched them up and put them in my jacket pocket. They've been in my pillowcase ever since."

"How did you know they were mine?"

"No disrespect to Mama D, but I knew they were yours, especially once I got a good look at them. I had a crush on you too," he said with a shy smile.

Jules opened her mouth to correct him, but she thought better of it. Those lavender panties really weren't hers. Lavender was Helene's favorite color, and Jules never had any lavender panties. *I'll tell him one day,* she thought.

"Shut. Up. Don't patronize me, Eli. Are you making fun of me?"

"Okay, it wasn't a crush so much as that…you were my first love. The first love, the only girl…I've *ever been in love with.*"

What the hell? Jules glared at him while trying to drive. He knew that look on her face.

"I swear," Eli said, raising his hands for emphasis. "I've been in love with you since the summer before you started high school. I was at your house when your mom brought you home from the airport after you'd spent the summer in Miami. You had more of a tan than I'd ever seen you with—you were glowing. Actually, come to think of it, it really happened the first time I saw you dance. I went to keep Chris company, and I left entranced by my best friend's baby sister. That was the Christmas before you went to Miami. I thought you were...perfect, and nobody else ever measured up."

Although Jules had heard him, she couldn't process what he had said, much less form words. And she was trying to drive, for crying out loud. Eli didn't look like he was joking, but Jules was trying not to look at him, as she was concentrating on merging on to Interstate 84.

"You can't be serious," she finally said, as she was driving at a comfortable speed of seventy miles an hour.

"I am," he said adamantly, "but why do you say that? Are you seriously telling me you can't tell the way I feel about you? I can't keep my mind off you, much less my hands or my lips. You were the last person I expected to encounter two weeks ago, and I've been trying to figure out how to tell you all this without freaking you the fuck out."

"Eli, you've dated beauty queens and models—literally, not figuratively. That one girl was Miss Teen Mass right?"

"Yeah, she was, but like I said, you had my heart. You have to remember, I've known you longer than I haven't. We had the same sense of humor, and you always tried to keep up with the boys because you wanted to play too—you couldn't always do it, but you tried. I liked that you did your own thing. A lot of people liked you, but you only had a few friends."

"Yeah, I was never the most popular," Jules admitted.

Eli shook his head. "I wouldn't say that. At the very least, you were popular by association. But you didn't buy into all the bullshit…and you always made me laugh. I'm astonished that you'd think I wasn't or couldn't be attracted to you."

"Well, that makes what I have to tell you just that much harder. You're right—I am avoiding something downtown. It's really someone. He works at O'Shea and Moore."

"Why are you avoiding him?"

"What did you do for winter break of your junior year of college?" Jules asked.

"I don't know. That was almost ten years ago. What does that have to do with—" he started.

"That winter…I was raped," she interrupted, as tears formed in her eyes.

"What?" Eli exclaimed, as the words seeped into his brain.

"I was drugged, beaten, raped, and I almost died—"

"What?" Eli repeated.

"But then the guy whose bed I was tied to pulled my panties out of my mouth so I wouldn't choke on my own vomit."

"Oh, my God, Jules…What?" Eli looked pained and sad-dened. *Who the fuck did this? I can't just ask her…I'm sure she'll tell me when she's ready.*

"Please stop saying 'What?'" Jules said, slightly agitated.

"Sorry. Please tell me they got the guy," Eli said, feeling sick.

"Right, counselor, because this is a perfect world we live in," Jules said sarcastically. She sighed before continuing. "There was a lot of physical evidence that was of no use, and I was buried under a pile of coats and clothes. The case never went to court; there never were any suspects, so there was no one to prosecute. He obviously used a condom because the only DNA on me was my own."

"DNA?" Eli seemed to be having trouble processing what Jules was saying.

"Yeah, blood and bodily fluids."

Eli turned his body toward hers, wanting to comfort her somehow.

"Did you have Mr. Radcliffe for government and econ?"

Eli nodded.

"So then you had to do the crazy end-of-the-semester project?"

"Oh, yeah, that shit was so tedious," Eli remembered.

"It was the Saturday after I turned that project in. Chris was having a huge cookout at his frat house because Boston College's football team was in the playoffs. We both convinced Ma that I'd be okay there. The problem was…we knew *him,* so he didn't seem threatening when he showed up at the party. The only thing I can figure is that he was mad because I'd gotten away from him twice."

"What do you mean 'gotten away from him'?"

"Two weeks before my senior year of high school started, he asked me out. I was still sixteen, and my parents didn't let me date. Group activities were allowed but no one-on-one dating. He was going back to Dartmouth for his senior year, and he practically pleaded with my mom to let him take me out before he left. When my mom told me he had asked her, she actually used the word 'pleaded.' Can you believe that? Anyway, he and I went to dinner and had about an hour to kill before the movie started. He drove down by the water. We started kissing—remember now, I was sixteen and this really was my first date—and he started putting his hands in all the wrong places, and I panicked. He called me a baby and said something like 'It's a shame you look like a woman but act like a little girl.'"

Jules exhaled deeply then continued. "So we started kissing again, and this time he tried to put his body on top of mine. I opened the door and slid out from underneath him. He got so pissed that he slammed the car door shut and threw my purse out the window and drove off." She sipped on her tea to soothe the lump in her throat.

"I walked inside the first open door I could find. It was a coffee shop, I think, and I called my friend Bethany to come get me. She took me home. When I got there, my ma and dad weren't home, so I headed upstairs and went to bed. The next day he sent flowers with a note, apologizing. I told my ma he wasn't nice, and I didn't like him. She didn't press it. I tossed the card and gave her the flowers."

"Fast-forward to December," Jules continued, "I was in the basement of the school library, putting the finishing touches on my project for Mr. Radcliffe's class. I had my earbuds in and my back turned to the elevator. I stood up and stretched, and he was right behind me. He spun me around to face him and pinned me against the wall. He said, 'I got you now' and put his hands up my shirt. I was trying to fight him off me when the elevator bell dinged. Mr. Stern, the library director, was bringing some items down to the storage area. The ding distracted the guy long enough for me to get to the elevator and close the doors. I think the only thing that saved me that day, besides Mr. Stern, was the renovation that was being done to the stairs. He couldn't use the stairs, and by the time the elevator got back down and up again, I was gone."

As Jules had asked, Eli remained silent while she told her story. But his brain was working overtime, trying to figure out who had done this unspeakable thing.

"I went straight home and didn't say a word to my parents about it. The next day, I went back to the library to retrieve my project, turned it in on Friday, and went to the party on Saturday. Maybe an hour or so after I got there, he showed up; I remember that much. Some of the details are still fuzzy, and most of the specifics that I know have been told to me. I do remember him approaching me at the party and trying to talk or explain or apologize...whatever. He brought me a drink that I later figured out was spiked with ketamine. I didn't have that little detail emerge until about a year later while I was in therapy, explaining to a shrink what had happened. I was telling him about getting to the party, and then I said it, I said *his* name, that *he* gave me the drink, and then I had a complete meltdown. The last memory I have is sitting on the couch, watching the BC game. From there, apparently he took me upstairs and tied my hands to the headboard, with my body facedown. The doctor at the hospital I later went to believes he was punching me as he violated me. He forcibly entered me in both places and tore me from end to end." Jules exhaled, sounding defeated.

"I can't believe I'm telling you this, Eli," she continued. "This isn't general knowledge. The police know, and my immediate family knows, and a couple of friends, but nobody else. I mean, people know it happened—they just don't know it happened to me. The guy who found me refused to say a word to the press about who I was. The 'scum of the earth' was slick—he either knew what he was doing, or he got incredibly lucky. He obviously knew a few people at the frat house but not enough to be noticed since he didn't go to school there. He came, did what he did, and left. He must've been gone for a while by the time the guy found me. It was like he was never there, except I was beaten to hell and completely violated. The poor guy found me tied to his bed under a pile of clothes. My body was beginning to try to rid itself of the poison, so I was convulsing."

Eli was completely silent as he stared out the window. *We know him. He went to Dartmouth, and he works at O'Shea and Moore.* Eli was taking notes and filing them away for further analysis. Jules decided to let him process what she was telling him; it was a shit ton of unexpected information. It was just past 9:00 a.m., and they were about two hours away from the city. They had encountered very little traffic and were making good time.

Eli let out a long sigh. "Jules, will you tell me how badly you were hurt?"

"I will, since you asked, counselor, but you have to know that when we get to Nettie's, I'm going to smoke a joint, and I have one more thing to tell you later. I don't want to talk about it while I'm driving because it's the one thing that still makes me very sad sometimes," Jules said. "I remember waking up in the hospital while my mom was sleeping in the chair next to my bed. I had five fractured ribs and various lacerated and ruptured internal organs, and an incredible amount of internal bleeding, not to mention all the damage he did to my reproductive organs. That's why the doctor believes the scumbag beat me.

The ER doctor said he couldn't believe one person had done this to another. I spent the whole next week in the hospital—and I had surgery as soon as I got to the hospital…well, after the CT scan, where they got a good look at the ruptured organs and fractured ribs, and then another surgery to correct a complication." Jules paused and turned to look at Eli for a moment. "How you doing with all this? You okay?"

No! I'm not okay. Fuck no. I. Am. Not. Okay. I'm anything but okay. Who the fuck did this? Why didn't Chris tell me? He wiped his face with his hands, inhaled deeply, then exhaled. "I'll be better when I can hold you, and you can tell me everything. I have to admit, you were absolutely right."

"Oh, yeah, about what?"

"I definitely can't 'unknow' any of this," Eli admitted, feeling extremely sad—and angry.

"Remember that earth-shattering sex?"

Eli nodded.

"Hold on to it. We got down before you knew all this, so you have high expectations to continue to meet. Now let me get to the next part, because it's why I'm still alive."

"So the story starts to get better?" Eli asked.

Jules nodded. "It does. There's still some bad stuff ahead, but the worst of it is over."

They were passing through Norwalk, Connecticut, and ran into some traffic. It didn't take long before they slowed to stop. Eli leaned his body over to Jules and took her face in his hands. Before he kissed her, he said, "Please tell me who and what helped you, because I'm so grateful."

After he lightly kissed her cheek, he used his phone to see what the holdup was because they weren't far from the city. When they passed the accident, Jules concentrated on driving, and Eli craned his neck to see if he could figure out what had happened. It was very clear—one car had sideswiped another.

"The accident looked like it happened while they were both in motion. The driver at fault was probably texting," Eli said.

"This world is full of stupid fucking people," Jules snapped. "All right, back to my story," she continued. "This whole thing wasn't covered up per se—it's a matter of public record—but it was kept out of the media. I don't know how…I guess since I was a minor. My dad was already a congressman, and his reelection campaign was starting after the holidays, so there was no use drawing unnecessary attention when the police weren't going to be able to find out who did it anyway. The day I was released from the hospital, my whole family went to Miami; no way did I want to stay in Boston. I had enough credits to graduate from high school, and I was only going back to school second semester for two Advanced Placement classes. Those two classes would've given me six credit hours to start my freshman year of college. My parents told everyone I had started at the U of M early admission, when in fact I delayed attending for a year and a half. My whole family went on the trip to Miami because they were going to tell me good-bye and leave me there."

"Wow, that must've been hard on you," Eli said.

"It was harder for my parents. I moved in with my aunt Leslie and her partner, Jackie. Those two are basically the reason I'm alive. Leslie's my 'cool aunt.' She was the first person I ever smoked pot with."

"Your aunt? She gave you pot? How old were you?"

"I think I was fourteen, before everything happened, when I was down in Florida for the summer, visiting her and Jackie. There were two or three tropical storms, and the change in barometric pressure gave me migraines. I woke her up while I was sick, and that's what she gave me to help me feel better. And then I was hooked…for lack of a better word. She made me promise and swear, and promise and swear, that I wouldn't tell my parents. When she saw I was true to my word, she started rewarding me with weed when I got good grades."

"What do Leslie and Jackie do for work that allows them to use marijuana?"

"Leslie has an established dermatology practice, and Jackie's a local artist whose work has been presented in a number of different galleries. She also was awarded a grant that started a kids' after-school art program. Once that program got started, it stayed funded and has been going strong for about thirteen years. They're basically self-employed and don't have anyone to answer to. No one tests them for drugs, so they use chronic frequently. That's where Roberto comes in."

"The guy who taught you about wine and food?"

Jules nodded. "He owns several legitimate businesses in the Miami area: two three-star restaurants—well, he's the co-owner of both restaurants and the sommelier at one of them—two dry cleaners, a Latino grocery store, and two small convenience stores. All those businesses were crucial because they laundered drug money.

"Javi's dad—Jorge—and Roberto are brothers. They came to the US and worked as dishwashers in the sixties. They saw how lucrative selling drugs was, but they were smart. They used the money they made to start legitimate businesses. Once they'd established their first legal business, they were good. They sold and distributed marijuana and cocaine in the beginning, and pills later on, I think. They bought the restaurant where they had started out as dishwashers. I don't know how they survived, because they got caught a couple times, and I didn't ask. They built an empire. Roberto came to Jackie and Leslie's at least once a week, if not more, and he always brought their green when he came.

"Things came to a boiling point about seven or eight months after I got there. Up until then, I'd been hard to deal with, and that's putting it mildly. All I know is Leslie and Jackie must really love me to have put up with my ass. Anyway, when Roberto arrived at the house one night, he realized he had forgotten the weed and called his nephew, Javier, to bring it. I was in rare form that night because I'd just been told I needed another surgery. My spleen had been damaged and repaired once but wasn't working properly. I was blinded with madness, seeing as how this was still inter-rupting and fucking with my life. So when Javi showed up with the goods, he knocked, and I opened the door. He just stood there looking at me, so I said something like, 'You just going to stand there or you coming inside?' He walked in, mumbling something in Spanish; I closed the door and said, 'Roberto, your errand boy is here.' Leslie reprimanded me for my comment then introduced us to each other. Again I was rude, and Leslie and Jackie scolded me, so my smart ass said, *"Lo siento. Parece que me quieres poner en mi sitio, deseas pegarme? Ahora que? Quieres que te la chupe? Te dolio los sentimientos chico?"*

"Jules, seriously, you offered him head because you were mean to him?"

"I said I was sorry too, but I told you I was in full melt-down mode. I grabbed the green and went to my room. Javier just stared a hole in my back as I walked out of the kitchen. As they sat at the table, Leslie gave him a quick synopsis of what had happened to me in Boston. About a week later, I had the surgery to remove the part of my spleen that wasn't working. Three weeks later, I was in rehab—correction: a mental rehabilitation clinic—and started taking a combination of antidepressants, only after my system had completely detoxed from all the drugs I was taking. That shit sucked—that was the whole first month."

"What prompted that?" Eli asked.

"Jackie was the one who found me, nearly overdosed, fully clothed in the shower with the water on full blast."

"Overdosed?" Eli's eyebrows shot up.

"Not on purpose, I promise. I told you I was self-medicating."

"What did she do?"

"Jackie called Leslie first, and Leslie told her what to do while she stayed on the phone and put her Jaguar's engine through its paces getting home. Somehow Leslie managed not to get a ticket while driving at breakneck speed. The two of them decided right then that they had let me work everything out on my own long enough, since what I was doing obviously wasn't working. That's why I didn't start at U of M for eighteen months. I had gone almost a full year with very little help, which quickly gave way to my self-medicating. After that, I received inpatient psychiatric treatment for four months. Somebody there started calling me 'Jules,' and it stuck. By this point it was creeping up on a year since that whole mess, and I really needed help."

"Ah, that's where 'Jules' came from. You went nearly a whole year with no help?" Eli asked.

"No, not completely. I saw a therapist, but halfway through our sessions, her partner took over because my therapist took a job as a professor at a local two-year school. I didn't really like him, so I stopped going and started self-medicating: weed, Valium, Vicodin—I've never really been a drinker. I just wanted the pain to stop. I felt like my body hurt all the time."

"Is the good part coming anytime soon?" Eli asked as they drove into the city.

Jules nodded. "I'm getting there. Toward the end of my treatment, the patients went through a sort of twelve-step thing."

"Like for alcoholics?"

"Yes, most people in recovery use the twelve steps to help put their lives back together. When it came time to make amends, I needed to apologize to Javier for the way I'd spoken to him. Which meant I had to call him and ask him to come over, and I was going to have to explain the stuff I told you; it's sort of like what people do before Yom Kippur. While I was telling him about the party at the frat house, I told him *who* gave me the drink, and then I lost it. I folded myself into a fetal position on the floor and cried. To my surprise, Javier stayed with me throughout my entire meltdown. According to Leslie, he didn't flinch. To my utter shock, he continued to visit and frequently attended my outpatient therapy sessions with me."

"He's the one who brought you back from the edge," Eli said.

"Yes, and it wasn't fun or easy. I definitely felt like more trouble than I was worth, because I wasn't what you'd call emotionally stable. I think Javier had a different opinion of me than he had of most women, especially after I apologized to him. Most of the women he encountered, I learned, wanted something from him: money, drugs, jewelry, or dick—which usually led to any of the previous items. I didn't want anything from him, except to apologize, and he didn't think I liked him, at least not at first. It wasn't that I didn't like him…I was angry and hurt. For whatever reason, I was fulfilling some emotional need for him. I think he liked feeling that he was taking care of me, protecting me. So he did his best to make me feel safe and help me learn to trust him…but the one thing I couldn't do was sleep with him, and he didn't push. He didn't even kiss me on the lips for like two months."

"Yeah, well…I didn't kiss you for like fifteen years," Eli said with a smile.

"It's not a competition, Eli. What is it with you athletes? Damn it." She shook her head.

Eli placed a gentle hand on her knee. "So what do I have to do to get you to trust me?"

"Eli…you've had my trust since I fell out of that tree when we were kids and you went and got your dad. Remember that?"

"I do," he said, as a smile went wide across his face. "You broke your left arm."

"You didn't know how to help me, but you knew someone who did. You were taking care of me." She smiled back at him. "Anyway, I had a full-time bodyguard, Bibiano, courtesy of Javier. He went with me to all my college classes, dropped me off at my front door every afternoon, and accompanied me to work each night. As an added bonus, Bibiano was a personal trainer, which worked in my favor because we ate in restaurants a lot, and he helped me maintain my weight with training sessions. And he also accompanied me when I went out with Javi. While we were out, Javi was regularly approached by random women. To say Javi had a healthy sexual appetite is an understatement."

"We weren't exclusive, but we'd been seeing each other, spending time together—whatever you want to call it—for about two months when he kissed me. He took his time with me—"

Eli cut her off. "Jules, please don't give me the blow by blow. I can't take the thought of another man touching you."

"Okay, you don't get to say that to me," Jules said a bit brusquely. "You can think it all you want, but you can't say it, seeing as how many women you've had your way with. The opposite sex has never been a challenge for you, and I don't like thinking about you with other girls either, but at least you've never seen me with another guy. I've seen you with several different girls."

"That's because you had my heart, and I had to distract myself because I couldn't have you."

Jules rolled her eyes. "Anyway, I'd been a hostess at one of Roberto's restaurants for about six months, and I was getting ready for work one day when Roberto called and asked me to stop by his house. He said he needed a specific tie or shoes or something. First, let me explain this family. The house took up an entire block, seriously. Three generations lived under one roof. The place had two wings and twenty something rooms. I walked into the wrong room and saw Javi getting his dick sucked."

Eli raised an eyebrow. "What did you do?"

"I covered my eyes, apologized profusely, and got the hell out of there."

"What did *he* do?"

"He came after me, came to the restaurant. He tried hard not to make a scene, but he was furious—more at himself really. He apologized, repeatedly, and begged me to talk to him. I smiled at him and told him he wasn't my boyfriend, and he had nothing to apologize for. His whole demeanor changed, like I had hurt his feelings, and he tried to argue. I thanked him for helping me feel safe and reassured him that we were close because he was an integral part of my recovery and said he had nothing to be sorry for. He sent flowers and gifts just so I'd call and ask him to stop, and he came to the restaurant every night. This went on for a little while, until Javier's cousin, Marco, came to see me. Marco made Bibiano answer a few questions in front of me, and then he made Bibiano swear that this meeting between the three of us never happened."

"What's that supposed to mean?

"Marco didn't want Bibiano to tell Javi that the three of us had talked, because ultimately it was Marco who persuaded me to talk to Javi. Up until then, we hadn't spent any time alone together. I'd have dinner with Javi at the restaurant but nothing else. I always told him I was busy with school, and I worked out a lot, thanks to Bibiano. I'd do my cardio while he did his killer workout, and then he'd cool down while he trained me."

"What did Marco tell you?"

"He told me that regardless of whatever happened, I needed to forgive Javi because he hadn't been his 'primo' in weeks. All he did was go to work and go home—no strip clubs, no partying, nothing. Marco said Javi wouldn't tell him what happened; all Javi would say was that he 'fucked up.' I told him nothing had happened. Marco said he didn't believe me and asked me to please see Javi. So I did. Again, Javi was incredibly apologetic. He told me he missed me and said he didn't like that I'd said he wasn't my boyfriend. I told him we'd never had a conversation about being in a relationship, and I assured him he didn't want to be in a relationship with me, and I didn't want to stand in his way of being with someone else he was more attracted to. He argued and told me I couldn't tell him that we weren't in a relationship and that he didn't want to be with me. I tried to tell him I couldn't give him what he wanted or needed sexually. He promised to take things slowly with me and said eventually I would want it, and he would be the one. And that's what happened. We were together until about a year ago."

"What happened a year ago?"

"Javier's family had legit businesses, but they were also into organized crime. I don't know specifically what happened, but that was for my benefit, according to Javi. So he disappeared about a year ago, and like I told you before, I honestly have no knowledge of where he is."

"Probably somewhere exotic that doesn't extradite to the US," Eli said, repeating her words to her.

"Right," Jules said, as she turned left on to Canal Street in Manhattan. "Okay, we're going to have to pause this conversation because I've never actually driven in the city before, and I'm completely…intimidated right now."

Eli picked up a piece of paper from the center console. "Your directions say to take Canal to Broadway. Then Broadway to NY-9A north and then to West 79th. But from West 79th, you have to turn left on to Amsterdam, and West 81st is the second right."

"Be prepared to say that again, since I think we're only on Broadway right now…I think."

"Do you plan on driving much when you live here?"

"Just to the grocery store really," Jules said. "I also thought that when I move here, I could go out late at night and just drive around, because I figure the traffic will be lighter than during the day. Once I'm more comfortable, maybe I'll drive in the day, but driving at night also will make sure the car gets cranked every once in a while. The whole point of driving here was to make sure the car, which my mother is so generously giving me, will fit in the garage of one of the brownstones I looked at six months ago."

"Okay. Get off on West 79th Street here," Eli said, pointing.

"We're almost there, and even with the wreck earlier, we made it before midday traffic."

They soon found Annette's luxury apartment building and her designated parking space. The doorman, having been alerted by Annette that they would be staying at her place, directed them toward the elevators. Jules unlocked the door as Eli walked in behind her and put their bags on the floor. It was a rather large apartment with a fantastic view; the living room had floor-to-ceiling windows that overlooked Central Park. The kitchen area and the living room were open, with no separation between the rooms. There were two bedrooms, each with its own full bathroom, behind the kitchen.

"I'll be right back. I have to pee—I'm about to bust. There's another bathroom just off the smaller bedroom," Jules said, as she took off for the master bathroom. A few minutes later, she made her way back to the kitchen. Eli was standing in the living room, looking out at Central Park. She walked up behind him and wrapped her arms around his waist.

"Hey, are you hungry? Annette said the fridge is fully stocked, and there's plenty of wine, but the ones on the bottom row of the rack are off limits," Jules warned.

Eli put his hands down over hers where they crossed over his torso, then put his arm around her to pull her over to his left side. "We do have a conversation to unpause," he reminded her.

"I haven't forgotten"—she looked up at him—"but I'm on pause until after dinner. I made reservations at Balthazar for seven," she said, before she got up on her tiptoes and kissed him.

"Wow, you are a master of diversion." He smiled into another kiss.

"I haven't heard any complaints from you," Jules said, "unless your complaint is that you think I'm a master at distracting you. Well, you distract me too. Why do you think I always kick you out of the office when I'm working? I told you: you exist; therefore you distract me. I'm not going to forget to finish our conversation, but Balthazar is one of my favorite restaurants, and I don't want to think about it until after dinner."

"Hey, did I tell you I love you?" Eli asked, as he knitted his brows together.

"I think you did in the car, but truthfully I was so astonished, I'm not actually sure."

"I love you, Jules. I'm in love with you, and I have been for an excruciatingly long time," he said, reaching down and embracing her. She wrapped her arms around his neck, and he picked her up and walked over and sat down on the couch.

Jules looked at him through those clear green eyes and bit her bottom lip as she grinned.

"I can't believe I'm going to say this out loud"—she paused for a moment—"much less *to* you, but I love you too, Eli. You're the only person who can make my heart beat a hundred miles a minute and make my knees weak at the same time," she admitted shyly.

The conversation that was on pause would stay on pause for the time being. Jules and Eli spent the next few hours talking about the little things they remembered about each other throughout the years. She was so distracted by the fact that he had said he loved her that she didn't even think about her weed. Weed was primarily a coping mechanism, but she never saw herself completely stopping. It was how she coped with life.

Jules couldn't help give Eli hell about all the girls who had hopelessly adored him. They just sat together, talking and sharing space, and looking out over the city. Eli just wanted to touch Jules, and in light of what he had learned on their trip into the city, he never wanted to leave her alone again.

At five o'clock, Jules jumped into the shower and got ready for dinner. Eli got dressed while she showered. He put on a soft-gray dress shirt and no tie, along with a pair black dress pants. He looked practically edible.

Eli didn't expect the sight that emerged from the bathroom. Jules was wearing a chartreuse vintage Diane von Furstenberg wrap dress that hung just above her knees, along with Leslie's fabulous Prada sandals with the three-inch heels. Her bangs were swooped to the left, out of her face, and her hair hung down, long and wavy, since she had wrapped a few random chunks around a curling iron. Her makeup looked fresh and natural; mascara thickened her lashes and defined her eyes, while her lip gloss gave shine to that perfect pout. Eli did his best to be present in the moment and drink in the sight of her.

"Wow," he whistled. "Are you trying to give me heart failure?"

"You like?"

"I…wow, yeah. I like."

"This is my fancy dress."

"It matches your eyes."

"It's my favorite color of green, both for weed and the actual color." She laughed. "Plus it's Diane von Furstenberg. I don't wear it often, but this is New York…and we're going to Balthazar."

"Are you planning on walking in those shoes?"

"I plan on wearing them, so yes, I'll walk in them, but I'll also carry a thin pair of sandals in my purse in case I need them."

"Do you want to walk?" Eli asked.

"Maybe a little after dinner. I thought we could catch a cab up here, and if we get there early, we can grab a drink at the bar."

Balthazar, located downtown on Spring Street near Broadway, was packed since it was a Thursday night. Eli was amazed Jules had a drink, especially because it wasn't red wine. It was a French 75—a delicious concoction of prosecco, gin, and sugared lemon—and he knew she was buzzed before she'd finished the first one. Thankfully they were seated at their table and ordering food before Jules finished her drink. She decided on mussels and pommes frites, and Eli ordered a hamburger with pommes frites. The pommes frites at Balthazar were absolute perfection. Eli ordered his hamburger medium with no mayo, for Jules, because he knew she would want to share and didn't like mayo. Without question he knew she was going to share her mussels with him too. Jules explained that the best part was sopping up the white wine sauce with the fresh-baked bread and some of those pommes frites.

Dinner was scrumptious, and Eli was certain Jules would want dessert. The crème brulée came out a few minutes after they ordered it. Jules had another drink during dinner then made a conscious choice to stop, since her lips felt numb. That was her indication to "say when."

Eli couldn't believe how relaxed she seemed; he wasn't sure whether it was the French 75s or what. Then again, this amazing woman sitting in front of him was relieved. She was free here, because there was no way she was going to encounter *him* anywhere in this city.

As they walked out of the restaurant, Eli put his arm around Jules's waist and guided her body toward his. It was a possessive gesture that made her giddy inside. They walked two blocks and came upon St. Patrick's Old Cathedral on Mulberry Street. He pulled her hand in the direction of the stairs up to the doors of the church.

"What are we doing in here, Eli?" Jules whispered, as he opened one of the church doors.

"I have a confession to make."

"Jews don't go to confession," she managed before he dragged her into a confessional. Thankfully, it was unoccupied on the other side; there was no priest to hear Eli's confession. It didn't matter anyway—this confession was for Jules. He sat down on the bench and pulled her down on top of him.

He placed his hands on both sides of her face and said, "I'm confessing to you that everything you told me scared me to death, but it doesn't scare me away from you." He barely got the words out of his mouth when he felt her lips meet his.

After a quick, sweet kiss, Jules said, "Thank you. I accept that. Now let's get outta here before we get caught."

They quietly left the church and hailed a cab.

Chapter 9

*J*ules was sitting in the back of the cab, experiencing con-
flicting emotions. She felt happy, but she also knew Eli
was expecting to unpause their previous conversation. That
knowledge was making her nauseous. To make matters worse,
when they arrived at Annette's apartment building, the elevator ride seemed to take forever. When they got to the apartment, Jules unlocked the door, and Eli followed her inside
and closed the door behind him. Keep in mind, Jules was
drunk (not sick drunk—more happy drunk, charged with a
fair amount of liquid courage). Eli was sporting a good buzz
as well and wasn't expecting Jules to push his body backward
toward the door. She had caught him off guard, which was
the only reason she was able to do it.

It happened quickly. As soon as Eli had faced her after he
had locked the door, she had put her hands on his chest and
pushed him backward. When he was sandwiched between the
door and Jules's body, she crushed her lips into his. Despite
his confession, she knew the last bit of what he wanted to
know might end this romantic relationship even before it
began, so as a precaution, she expressed her feelings by sucking on his tongue and bottom lip. She broke away from Eli
while he was still trying to kiss her.

"I'm going to change my clothes and roll a joint. Feel free to open a bottle of wine if you want, but I'm good, and remember not to open anything on the bottom row. I'll be right back."

After Jules put on a gray tank top and a pair of small black shorts, she pulled out two plastic prescription bottles filled to the brim with beautiful chartreuse-green weed. Then she located the glass pipe and lighter that were in her makeup bag. On her way back into the living room, she stopped in the kitchen for a large glass of filtered water.

Alcohol and weed were never a good combination for her. It was one or the other but not both. However, considering what she was about to tell Eli, she needed her weed. Her brain was quantifying her food-to-alcohol ratio; she figured she had eaten enough food to soak up two drinks, or at least enough so that she wouldn't get sick from mixing alcohol and weed. The water would help too.

Eli was lying on the couch in his boxer briefs, searching for something to watch on Amazon Prime. Jules sat down near his feet and packed the bowl.

"I thought you were going to smoke a joint?"

"Found my glass in my makeup bag. Listen, I don't actually know if you've ever gotten high before, but I like to think you have."

"I have indeed. Why?"

"You definitely will want to now. Trust me…Let's smoke a bowl, and you can ask me anything you want, and then I'll unpause our conversation and tell you the rest."

"In retrospect I wish we'd had this in the car," he said, as he lit the bowl.

"I did have it in the car," she replied.

He looked at her. "You know what I mean."

"Nothing makes it easy, but somehow Mary Jane helps," Jules reasoned.

Eli handed her the pipe and exhaled. At the end of his exhale, he coughed a little as Jules inhaled deeply.

"Hit it again and ask me what you want to know," Jules said, seeming to give him permission.

"You know I want to know who raped and beat you, but I'm not going to ask you that directly and expect you to answer me. You told me we know him, he went to Dartmouth, and he works at O'Shea and Moore, right?"

"Yes, counselor." Jules was amused at Eli's examination tactics and how he seemed to turn them on automatically. She inhaled, cleared the pipe, then lit it again, hit it, and passed it back to Eli.

"Son of bitch," Eli said, as if he were lost in thought. "It was Denny Griffin, wasn't it?"

Jules nodded. "You can't ever say his name out loud again, okay? You wanted to know why I don't like being downtown, so now you know. Just promise me that if we're ever out in public and we…encounter him, please don't let me fall on my ass or my face."

"Yeah, okay. I'll keep you upright. Got it. Was that what you were going to tell me when we unpaused? That he did it?"

"Nope, but every day I walk out of my parents' house and pray that I won't run into him. Being back in Boston has my anxiety off the charts, and I can't control it. That's why I vape so much weed. Eli, I need you to promise me that no matter what I say, you'll weigh both sides of the situation thoroughly before you make any decisions."

"Decisions about what?"

"Whether or not to go ahead with our relationship."

"Jules, let me state this for the record, in case I wasn't explicit the first time: I'm in love with you, and I have been for longer than I haven't. There's no decision to make…You're mine, and I'm yours, babe. You and me are a 'we.'"

"Really? When did you and me become a 'we'? *We* haven't discussed any part of this. You have a whole life in Boston. There are so many moving parts to this, and I can't expect you to just pick up and move your life. Besides, what I'm going to tell you is something you have to know, and please understand that I'm not saying this to you lightly, and I rarely ever talk about it. There was so much damage done internally and to my 'undercarriage' that I can't…I can't have children," Jules said, as tears dripped from her eyes.

Eli wrapped her in his arms and pulled her to him. A few tears escaped his eyes as well. They seemed to slip out before he could suppress the gut-wrenching emotions he was feeling. He would save that meltdown for a later time. He cupped her face with one hand and held her close to him with the other.

"That's an obstacle we'll face together," he said softly.

"No, you have to make sure it's something you can live with…and without. It's for real. Biological children aren't a possibility…There's no 'maybe' about it."

"There's adoption, surrogacy—and that's all beside the point. Tell me you don't want to be with me," Eli said, sounding perturbed.

"It's not about that. Of course I want to be with you, but you won't be able to have children with me…ever. I don't think your parents are going to be okay with that," Jules nearly exclaimed. "And that's just a waste of good genetics, if you ask me." She chuckled, trying to make him smile. He shook his head and looked away from her, clearly not appreciating her humor.

"Eli, I know having this knowledge is hard. I vaped an unusually large amount the day I realized I was going to have to tell you about this. I actually thought about buying a cigar, busting out the guts, and smoking a blunt straight to the head just at the thought of having to tell you. I haven't smoked a blunt in probably five years. One day you'll be able to look at me, and this won't be the first thing that comes to mind. I don't think about it every day anymore…but I also don't go to baby showers either. This one thing makes me the saddest, and it's all because of a Mother's Day project from first grade."

"A few years after this happened," she continued, "my ma sent me a box of my old stuff she didn't want to throw away, but she wanted it gone because she was on a cleaning tirade. You know how she gets. Anyway, there was a book in there that each kid had to make for their moms for Mother's Day. One of the pages asked us what we wanted to be when we grew up. I said I wanted to be a ma just like mine because she was the best," Jules said, tears streaming from her eyes.

"Jules, baby…please don't cry. My heart can't take it." Eli looked frantic. "You'll be a mama, I promise, and you'll be just as good a mama as yours."

Jules took a deep breath. "Just promise me you'll think about this later, because it's a major life decision."

"No, Jules, I won't. If I agree to that, then it implies that a possible outcome of this would be our not being together, and I'm not going to entertain that thought at all."

"But—" she tried to argue.

"I'm not wavering on this, Ms. Dempsey. Answer this question for me—a simple yes or no will do. Do you want to be with me?"

"You know I do," she said matter-of-factly.

"Then we'll handle all the rest together," he said, as he gently cupped the sides of her face in his hands.

Conceding to his stubbornness, Jules chose to drop it. This was all too much. How in the world was she going to protect herself when this mess went sideways? She tried not to be pessimistic, but she wondered if she could keep Eli truly happy.

"Let's take that bowl to the huge bed in the master bedroom," Eli suggested. "I want to hold you, and we can smoke another bowl and start *House of Cards* since you said you never got to it."

He stood up and led Jules to the bedroom. "Are you okay?" she asked, as they lay down in the middle of the king-size bed.

"I don't know how to answer that," Eli said, lighting the bowl and inhaling. "You told me something I can't change or do anything about. Nope, nothing I'm feeling is okay. My woman, my love, just told me that some piece of shit who pretended to be our friend hurt her in a way that's indescribable," Eli said, stroking her hair.

"I'm your woman, huh?" Jules asked shyly.

"Damn straight." He smiled at her. "Yes, love. Didn't I say that already? I love you, Jules. I'm so in love with you that I feel like I'm going to burst. Do you want to be my woman?" he asked, almost hesitantly.

"Since I'm in love with you too, it wouldn't make much sense for me not to be," she said with a smile, "but thank you for asking."

"Good." He rubbed his nose against hers, and their lips met. If his smile made her melt, his kiss turned her into vapor, and he loved kissing her. "Would you think I'm a horrible person if all I wanted to do was lick your entire body and make you giggle and scream my name?"

"Truthfully," Jules said, "I was terrified you wouldn't feel that way ever again."

"Oh, Jules, baby, no…oh, no. But I might be a little gentler sometimes. I'm so sorry you ever felt that way or thought that my knowing this would change the way I feel about you."

"It's still a lot to handle," she exhaled through struggled breaths as he kissed his way from her jawline down her neck, his fingers diligently working at removing her tank top.

"Can we" (kiss) "deal with" (kiss) "that together too?" (kiss) he asked, putting light kisses on her flesh and intermittently nibbling her pebbled, petal-pink nipples.

"This might help: you don't ever have to wear a condom again." Jules smiled weakly as she pulled his shorts down from his waist.

Eli sat back on his knees, pushed his shorts all the way down, and dragged her shorts down too. Jules sat up and pushed his tank top up over his torso, and then Eli pressed his body into to hers. His right hand wandered to the bare folds between her legs.

"I really like the wax…if I didn't tell you before." Eli's lips crashed into hers as he inserted two fingers into her warm, moist spot. Jules was more than ready, and Eli couldn't get enough of the way her body responded to him.

"Please, Eli," came her breathy request.

"Please, what, baby?" he whispered into her ear before he bit down on her earlobe.

"Take your fingers out."

"Am I hurting you?"

"No, I just like your cock better," she teased.

"Are we listing our favorite body parts?"

"They're all my favorite," she said before he kissed her.

Once their lips met, they didn't part. Eli did as she asked and took his fingers out, then filled her completely, slowly. Although he'd had numerous sexual encounters, this was entirely different. Their first couple of times having sex, it was hot, fun, exhilarating. That was her intention, as it was a fantastic diversion from the conversation he'd wanted to have. But this was the first time Eli ever *felt* like he was making love.

"Look at me, Jules," he said before he kissed her, looking her in the eyes. She looked back at him and saw all his feelings staring back at her. Eli did love her, and Jules saw it…and she felt it with every thrust of his hips, which met her warmth continuously. He kept his eyes open and locked on hers as she nipped at his bottom lip. His strong hands caressed her body while his thick cock drove her to her first orgasm of the night.

"Elijah! Don't stop…I'm coming!" Jules screamed.

"I love you, Jules," Eli said, as he brought his mouth down over hers and increased his pace to hasten her climax. "And I love when you scream my name," he told her, his quickened pace matching her heavy breathing. "Say it, baby…Tell me you love me," he encouraged her.

"I…I love you, Eli," Jules declared, as her walls clenched his cock and her body trembled as she moaned. Just then, Eli pulled his throbbing, erect penis out of its new favorite spot and replaced it with his face. Jules didn't have the thought capacity to object. She didn't need to anyway. His tongue was magnificent, and he wasn't shy about using it. He sucked and licked her aching bud, which had her bucking her hips and experiencing a simultaneous orgasm. She giggled uncontrollably and reached for Eli's face. He licked his way back up the length of her body until he reached her mouth. Eli was doing his best to slow down, but it was maddening to Jules.

Jules looked up at him. "Eli, come inside me."

"Jules, I've never—" he started.

"Me either, but I love you. Don't pull out," she told him.

Eli buried himself inside her. "Oh, Jules, baby, you feel so good wrapped around me," he breathed into her neck. He knew he wasn't going to last, so he stuck his hand between her legs and gently rubbed her super-sensitive bud. Several seconds of that unbearable pleasure sent Jules over the edge once more, and she took him with her. Eli experienced pure ecstasy, and they experienced another "first" together.

"Oh...shit!" Eli growled as he laid his head on Jules's chest while his semihard cock continued to fill her throbbing pussy. "I have to amend my previous statement."

"What's that?" Jules asked, oblivious to what he was talking about.

"The first time we made love...I said it was the best sex of my life. I need to add 'so far' to that, because that shit right there...that was unbelievable," he said, as he closed his eyes and smiled.

"I'm just glad I got to be some kind of first for you," Jules said, as her fingers lightly brushed the back of Eli's neck while he rested on top of her.

"Ms. Dempsey, I'll address that statement tomorrow. Right now I'm going to clean up, and we both need some sleep," Eli said, striding to the bathroom for a wet cloth. He returned with a hand towel for Jules. She cleaned the stickiness from between her legs, folded the mess to the inside of the towel, and tossed it toward the bathroom.

Eli, in all his naked glory, climbed back into bed and pressed his body against hers. He needed to touch her. Ever since the day he'd seen her sitting in her dad's office, she was no longer a want. Jules had become his most recent need. Besides, he had loved her way back, when he first had figured out what love was.

he morning came before Jules was ready, but she did come to the city for a specific reason. She planned on making her career in New York, and she needed a place to live. As she had told Eli the day before, she had driven Helene's BMW because she needed to see if it would fit in the garage. In her opinion, there was no reason to take the car if she didn't have a place, besides the street, to park it.

Jules wasn't extravagant—yes, she had come from money, but most people would never know that. Her parents had raised their children with morals, ethics, and manners. The Dempseys had taught their children to conserve, preserve, and be thankful for what they had. So the simple fact that Helene was *giving* her daughter her BMW X3, which had been paid for and barely had 60,000 miles on it, made Jules incredibly appreciative. As far as Jules was concerned, as long as she had the car regularly serviced, she would get decades of use out of her new ride. So her goal was to find a place with a garage large enough to accommodate it.

The first property Jules and Eli looked at was on the higher end of the budget she had set, so she just looked around patiently and let Lorraine go through her spiel. The problem was that it was expensive and also needed some work. Eli knew by Jules's silence that she wasn't even considering it. The apartment faced the Hudson River and wasn't too far from Annette's place. It had started out as a single apartment, but then the previous owner had bought the apartment above. Neither apartment was in great shape. To top it off, it was located at 160 Riverside Drive, which was quite a distance from her office.

"Why don't you two go up to the top floor and look around? I'll answer any questions you have when you make your way back down," Lorraine called behind them as they headed up the stairs.

Lorraine looked every bit her job. She wore tailored suits—this one was red—and low heels. Her chin-length black hair was elegantly styled, and her big, friendly brown eyes were welcoming.

"You don't even care about this one, do you?" Eli asked when they were out of earshot.

"Nah, but what else do we have to do right now?"

"Oh, I can think of about forty-six things to do to you, and that's just off the top of my head," Eli said, wiggling his eyebrows and pulling her to him by her waist.

"Easy, counselor. Besides, we only have two more places to look at, and then we have the rest of the day to ourselves. And you never know, I might see some things in some of these apartments that'll give me ideas for my place," she said, as they walked from room to room. "I have no idea how I'd fill all these rooms with furniture," Jules said, nearly cringing at the thought.

The next two apartments were worth seeing, but neither of them were contenders. Jules didn't think they felt like home, and they were a little farther away from work than she wanted. Only one of the apartments had a garage, and the building was a luxury one like Annette's place. This particular style of dwelling was what Jules had in mind originally. However, there was a property at West 67th and Columbus Avenue, a brownstone, that had been purchased as a short sale a few years ago, and now it was being foreclosed on, and Jules loved it, at least from the pictures she had seen. It too had a garage. She would take Eli to see it on Saturday and also make sure the car fit in the garage.

The night was warm—in the low eighties—and it was crazy humid, but a nice breeze cooled the air down a bit. That evening they went to Central Park for a free concert and took pizza for a picnic. They left the park around ten and made their way back to Annette's to shower off the sweat. As soon as Jules laid her head on Eli's chest, she fell fast asleep. Eli drifted off shortly after, holding the woman who held his heart.

On Saturday afternoon, all Eli could think was that Sunday was rapidly approaching. Oddly enough, after hearing what Jules had to tell him, he wasn't in a hurry to get back to Boston either. He was on high alert now that he knew what was scaring her or, more specifically, *who* was scaring her. Eli couldn't blame Jules in the slightest for not wanting to be in Boston; he just wanted to be with her wherever she chose to be. If that was New York, so be it. He wanted to make their last night of their first trip special and pleasurable. Jules had to help him find his way out of his thoughts while they were looking around the foreclosed brownstone.

He liked the brownstone just as much as she did and made sure to make suggestions that would make Jules aware that he could see himself living there…with her, of course. He piped up in one of the bedrooms. "This room would look good in a light-blue color with dark-blue and gray furniture," he said.

Jules stared at him in quiet amazement before saying, "You're going to need to warn me before you go all 'Martha Stewart' on me." Eli laughed and snaked his arms around her waist.

Admittedly it had been torturous for him to keep his hands to himself when he was in love with her when they were teenagers. But they were grown now, and he didn't care who saw them together, touching and kissing each other in New York—or in Boston for that matter. He didn't seem to care where they were when the mood struck. If he wanted to hold her hand or kiss her, he did. New York was bringing two beginnings for them. First, it was the official beginning of their exclusive relationship. Second, it was where they would spend their lives together.

Eli decided right then, in the brownstone, that he would talk to Jules's dad as soon as they got home on Sunday. Well, he would see his parents first, and then he'd talk to Jules's father. The visit with them would make the visit with Mr. D possible. He would to have to ask for Jules's father's permission; it was the respectable thing to do, especially since Mr. D had played an integral role in Eli's adolescence and adulthood. So many thoughts were running through his mind that he had forgotten they needed to eat. In fact, both of them had completely spaced out on eating lunch.

"It's almost five. How about we grab an early dinner and then have lots of yummy desserts after dinner wears off some?" Jules said, as she parked the BMW in Annette's designated parking spot.

"What were you thinking for dinner? Do you want to go out or stay in?" Eli asked.

"How does gourmet Chinese sound? There's a scrumptious spot in Midtown, and it might be early enough to get in on short notice. Is that okay with you?"

"Chinese sounds great. Let's see if we can go now."

"Okay. Let me make the call," she said, stopping in the main entrance to Annette's building while she called Chen's. "Hi. Good afternoon. Would you have any availability for two for dinner at six?" Jules looked at Eli, who looked hungry for her. "Great, the last name is Dempsey. Thanks so much. We'll see you at six."

"Do you think you'll last that long? We haven't eaten since breakfast," Eli reminded her.

"I thought we could walk there and take a cab back. It's only about thirty blocks from here, which is nothing. If we're walking and talking, I think I'll be fine, especially since we'll be moving in the direction of food—and it's fantastic food."

"Lead the way, Ms. Dempsey," Eli said with a smile.

"Oh, and if you see anything that strikes your fancy in the way of desserts, let's stop and get it," Jules said, smiling back.

"Let's not leave something as important as dessert to chance," Eli said, as he pulled out his phone to search for desserts in the area. On the way to the restaurant, they picked up four cupcakes, two cannoli, two slices of baklava, and six pieces of halva. They also got one large piece of turtle caramel cheesecake to split. Eli loved eating with Jules; she loved delicious food and had excellent taste.

They enjoyed as much as they could eat that Chen's had to offer: buttery scallops and perfectly wrapped shrimp dumplings, and the crispy orange duck was exquisite. Although Eli enjoyed dinner, he couldn't wait to get Jules back to Annette's apartment.

The cab ride back to the apartment was the beginning of their last night in the city. When Eli had gotten into the car with Jules back in Boston, he had no idea this weekend would so revealing. His plan was to keep Jules awake late into the night then sleep until late in the morning. Although the elevator was slightly crowded when they stepped in to go up, Jules and Eli only noticed each other.

After Jules let them into the apartment, Eli put the desserts in the refrigerator. She locked the front door then met him in the kitchen. He felt as if he'd accomplished a major feat today by not taking her into every dark corner for a little "daytime delight." He had resisted, but he didn't have to now.

"I need a shower before I can even think about dessert." Jules batted her eyelashes as she walked past him toward the bathroom in the master bedroom. This trip had been more stressful than she'd expected, and she wasn't sure how this new relationship was going to work, especially considering the traumatic events of her past, but she didn't want to think about that now. She just wanted to shower. Jules was undressing on her way to the bedroom, and Eli was trailing her.

"Would you mind if I joined you?" he asked, unhooking her bra. He placed light kisses on the back of her neck up to her hairline.

"Not when you ask like that," she exhaled.

He led her into the beautifully tiled bathroom. Warm sand colors, from light to dark, covered the bathroom from the floor to the middle of the wall. From the tile to the ceiling, the bathroom was painted a seafoam green that reminded Jules of the beach in Miami.

Eli turned on the hot water, and when he turned back around, Jules was completely naked. Her naked body had become a craving for him, and he planned to do as much as he could to express that. Eli wasn't sure when the next time would be when he would see her so free and unfettered. He was catching a glimpse of an energy in her that he couldn't get enough of.

As Jules opened the glass shower door, hot steam billowed out, flooding the spacious bathroom. She stepped in, and Eli got in behind her and closed the door. He was hesitant, slow to touch her as the warm water slid down her porcelain skin, instantly making her nipples hard. The tips of all ten of his fingers brought a rise of chills and goose bumps to the surface of Jules's skin.

Eli's tall, lean stature towered over her petite frame. She looked up at him with eagerness in her eyes while her hands grasped his waist. He cupped her face with his right hand and pulled her to him with his left.

"Eli…" she started.

"Yeah, baby?"

"I love you—with all of me. I have forever, and I will forever." Jules barely got the words out before his lips met hers.

Eli was coming unhinged physically, emotionally, mentally, and spiritually—and it was all because of this indescribable love he had for Jules.

Jules gently pushed his back to the wall and dropped to her knees in front of him. She stroked his fully erect manhood; when her perfect lips parted, his pinkish-brown head felt the warmth of her tongue. Eli closed his eyes and ran his hands through his short, dark hair as water rushed down his body; he was so thankful for the tiled wall that was holding him upright.

"Oh. Fuck. That feels…incredible," he managed as she took his cock farther down her throat. Eli fisted both hands in her hair while her head moved back and forth; her lips were wrapped around his luscious piece, sucking, licking, and stroking.

"Jules, Jules, baby…stop!" he nearly pleaded.

"What's wrong?" She was startled as Eli lifted her to her feet.

"As much as I want you to keep doing that, I've never been one for shower sex. It's a little too slippery for my liking. Let's wash up so I can finish what you started."

"Anywhere in particular?" Jules asked.

"I don't care if it's the counter, the floor, the bed—just not in the shower. Can I bathe you, love?"

"Everywhere?" she asked in surprise.

"Yes, love, everywhere. I'm going to clean your whole body so I can lick it from top to bottom and back again." Then he kissed her passionately.

She took her lips away from his. "We'll never get clean if you keep kissing me like that," she said with a chuckle.

Eli smiled as he kissed her then reached behind her to the shampoo bottle and managed a few pumps. The next thing Jules felt, besides his kissing her, was his soapy hands lathering her hair. After a few minutes, he backed her up under the steady stream of warm water to rinse her off.

"How about you let me take care of the rest, huh?" Jules asked.

"Where's the fun in that? Put some conditioner in your hair, and I'll bathe you."

Jules did as he suggested; she spread the conditioner through her hair while Eli lathered some soap in a washcloth. His touch was exquisite—soft and firm, purposeful yet wandering. As his lips met hers again, the only thought she could muster was that she was going to torture him in the very same way shortly. Eli backed her up under the water again and tossed the washcloth onto the bench behind him. Then he gently placed his soapy hand between her legs. He felt the heat radiating between her legs at his touch—this was for him...*he had done this to her.* After he was satisfied that her wanting pussy was clean, he cradled her ass with one hand and slipped his other hand around to the split of her ass. Jules wasn't expecting it, but as his hand moved up and down, she bucked her ass into his hands. Eli pulled the removable showerhead down and placed it between her legs to rinse her thoroughly.

"You taste so good—I have to make sure all I can taste is you."

If this is his version of talking dirty, I hope he never shuts up, Jules thought.

As Eli replaced the showerhead, Jules scooted behind him and picked up the soapy washcloth. With a devious tone, she said, "My turn." She used both hands to turn his body around so the steady stream of water hit his back. She used her free hand to further lather his deliciously sculpted body. His dick was rock hard the entire time. After he was thoroughly rinsed, she stepped out of the shower, wrapped herself in a towel, and turned her body toward his to put a towel around his waist. Then she pulled him to her with a seductive gesture.

He knew she was all his, and after she had declared her love for him yet again when they'd first gotten in the shower, he was experiencing a range of emotions he hadn't expected: a combination of love and fear.

The bed was less than ten feet from the shower. As Eli cradled the back of Jules's head, his nimble fingers massaged her neck as their lips met. When Jules backed up to the bed, Eli laid her down and pushed her legs up. Anticipation's a bitch, and Eli was testing her resolve, because Jules wanted to scream. She wiggled and giggled, partially because he was tickling her, and then she started anticipating the tickle.

Soft lips touched her aching bud. Eli's wet tongue licked and teased her clit before he reached up and wrapped his forearms around her thighs and pulled her to the edge of the bed. Jules was ready to lose control, and Eli could feel it.

His tongue entered her slick folds again, and it was mind-blowingly excellent. He certainly knew what he was doing. Satisfied that the bottom half of his face was soaked, he relented, stuck his index and middle fingers between her slick folds, and crooked them upward. He hit that bundle of nerves with the pads of his fingers. Jules was close, and Eli loved knowing that he had brought her there. He licked and lapped and pushed her rear up off the bed. Without hesitation he plunged his tongue between her butt cheeks. Although Jules gasped, trying to catch her breath, Eli didn't stop his relentless assault on her derriere.

"Flip over, baby," he grunted.

"Yeah, baby," she said breathlessly.

Eli bent forward and put his tongue right where it had been before—he loved licking her ass. Then he pulled his face back and pushed in from behind. Jules moaned, while Eli smiled, satisfied. He started out slowly, thrusting into her deeply. She pushed her ass toward him, meeting his thrust, taking every bit of him. Eli stuck his index finger in his mouth from knuckle to tip, and then he touched the unoccupied star. Jules pushed back a little, and that was all the encouragement he needed; he stuck his finger in her ass. She gasped, then moaned, then backed her ass up to him. He was gentle, but she felt like he was hitting her G-spot from the other side. His other hand gripped her ass as he quickened his pace, and he continued to slide his finger in and out of her ass while her fucked her pussy.

"Oh, baby, this shit is so damn good," he growled, then stopped for a moment. Jules spread her legs a little farther, pressing her chest into the bed, then moved back and forth on his cock.

"Mm-hmm," she responded, unable to form words. She felt a tightness in her ass that she'd never experienced before. Between Eli's finger in her ass and his enormous cock in her pussy, she was coming in every way possible.

"Eli…uh, Eli. Baby, oh, yeah," she moaned as she melted into him and the bed beneath them. Jules felt him release, long and hot inside her, as her orgasm rolled through her body.

"Roll over and lie on your back," Eli demanded. She fulfilled his request, and he plunged his semierect penis into her throbbing pussy. Jules looked up at him curiously.

"I just wanted to kiss you while I'm inside you," he said, before placing his lips to hers, and then she wrapped her arms around his neck. He pushed in once or twice, but even though he knew he was done, he didn't want to stop. Jules was the only place he felt out of control. Reluctantly he pulled his softening cock out of her slick pussy and rolled to his side. He lay beside her with his arm draped over her body, still trying to possess her.

"Hey, beautiful," he said with a smile as she recovered. "Was that okay?"

"Well, 'okay' isn't how I would describe it, but yes. Why?"

"I just wanted to make sure my playing with your ass was okay, and if it wasn't, I want you to be able to tell me," he said with a shy smile.

"You'd never do anything to hurt me, right?"

"Never," he said, lightly touching her face.

"Then I don't care how or where you touch me, but your finger is all you get there, because your dick is way too fucking big for my ass."

Eli threw his head back and laughed, and Jules leaned into his touch. Sleep came some time later, after they'd both cleaned up. They never got around to all those delicious desserts…because they were each other's dessert.

Chapter 11

On Sunday morning, Eli woke up with a feeling of dread, although he wasn't sure why. Boston was his home. No matter where he was in the world, he was always happy to get back home. Jules was still asleep, and he would have given anything to stay with her in New York for a couple of weeks. He got up out of bed, grabbed his phone, and walked out of the bedroom.

"'Morning, Mom. You up?" Eli asked, as he sat down on the couch, watching morning settle over the city through the large picture windows.

"I am. Your dad and I are working in the garden," Debra replied.

"Will you be home later this afternoon?"

"As far as I know, I should be. Why? Is everything okay?" Debra asked.

"I was just hoping to come by and see you and Dad when Jules and I get back to Boston later today."

"Well, if we're not here when you get here, you can use your key." Debra King knew her son, and she knew something was wrong.

"Okay, Mom. I'll call you when I'm near the house," Eli said quietly.

He hung up the phone then walked into the kitchen to turn on the coffee maker. He also found a measuring cup, filled it with water, and put it in the microwave so he could make Jules some tea. The return trip to Boston was inevitable, but she was going back as "his woman." All he wanted to do was take her to his apartment and make her scream his name while her fingers gripped his hair. The first thing he needed to do, though, was see his parents. They were going to make this better.

Jules was lying on her side, facing the door. Eli stood in the doorway, staring at her. The last seventy-two hours or so, plus the two weeks that had preceded it, had been…enlightening, to say the least. He lay back down beside her and traced her eyebrows and lips with his ring finger. Jules knitted her eyebrows together and barely opened her eyes as a wide grin grew on her lips.

"'Morning," she whispered.

Eli smiled back. "'Morning."

"What time is it?" she asked.

"A few minutes after nine. You hungry? I'm making you some tea."

"Wow. Thanks. I didn't know you were such a morning person," she said through heavy lids.

"I got up about twenty minutes ago. I was making coffee for myself and decided to make you some tea," he said, then kissed her on the forehead. "Now come on. Get up. Let's have our desserts for breakfast, and what we don't eat we can take with us."

"Yeah, yeah, all right. Give me fifteen minutes, and I'll brush my teeth, get dressed, and get my stuff together."

"You want me to drive? 'Cuz I will," he said with a smile.

"Actually, that would be great," she said, getting up.

After they got dressed, ate, and gathered their belongings, they left Annette's key on the counter and locked the bottom lock from the inside. When they got into the car, Jules texted Annette to thank her once again and let her know they were leaving. Eli drank his coffee, and Jules drank her tea. Jules texted her ma to let her know they were on their way home. Eli didn't really try to engage her in conversation until they were out of the city, since he was paying close attention to the traffic and the GPS on his phone.

Once they were on the road, they talked about the properties they had looked at over the weekend. Eli was determined to express his opinions regarding furniture, paint colors for different rooms, and even accessories such as couch pillows. They both loved the brownstone at West 67th and Columbus Avenue that was in foreclosure. Jules put her left hand on Eli's leg while he was driving, and he periodically covered her hand with his; he seemed content with that. They reminisced and listened to Snoop Dogg's *The Doggfather* on Sirius radio for a while, and then Jules found a downloaded audiobook on Eli's phone.

"You have Tina Fey's *Bossypants* on here? Have you listened to it yet?"

"I've had it on there for a long time, but I haven't listened to it."

"I can't believe it," she teased him.

"What? I dig her sense of humor."

Jules smiled. "Somehow that doesn't surprise me, but so do I."

"Somehow that doesn't surprise me either," Eli teased her.

They rode together in a comfortable silence. Tina Fey had each of them laughing out loud at her hysterical antics all the way back to Boston. He drove them straight to his place.

"Eli, can I use your bathroom since we made the four-hour trip without any stops?"

"Absolutely not. There are four unused bathrooms in my house, and three of them will stay that way," he said, as he put the car in park, "because I also have to pee. And like I said, you can't use any of my bathrooms," he added with a smirk.

"Really, Eli! You think this particular moment is the time to mess with me?"

"Truthfully, Jules, it's just as ridiculous as you asking me to use the bathroom at my house. Of course you can. Using the bathroom at my house is something you do…You don't ever have to ask. Ask before you delete something from the DVR; ask me for money; or ask me what we're having for dinner, but if it's something you'd do at your house, you can do it at my house," he said sincerely.

After Jules used the bathroom, Eli did everything to get her to stay. She teased him about being tired of her, but he debunked that comment. Eli tried to feed her, get her naked, and make love to her. He was attempting to make Boston *theirs;* he was trying to make her feel wanted so Boston wouldn't feel like such a sad place. Jules managed to avoid each of his efforts, however, so he walked her out to her car and told her to call him in the evening.

The Kings' backyard looked as if Debra had been out there getting a total-body workout, but yard work truly made her happy. Her summer garden was going to produce delicious vegetables. She also had been planting Japanese tea olive trees, which have the most pleasant sweet fragrance. Eli walked through the back door of the house where he'd grown up. His parents' house was a soft place for him to land.

He closed the door. "Mama, you home?"

"I'm in the den, honey," Debra called out.

Eli walked into the den to find his mom watching an episode of a documentary TV show about the history of New York City. She was sitting on the couch, looking freshly showered after her romp in the yard. Her short hair was tied up in a scarf, and she had on her glasses. Debra hated wearing glasses and only wore them when she was at home.

"Your garden looks like it's coming along nicely," he said, sitting beside her.

"Thanks. Did you see the new bushes?"

"The ones that line the sunroom?"

"Mm-hmm," she answered.

"I did. They look great. Where's Pop? Did he help you outside?" he asked, making small talk.

Debra smiled. "He did most of the heavy lifting. He's in his office, I think."

Eli just sat there and didn't say anything.

"Did you and Jules have fun in New York?" she asked, turning off the program she was watching.

"New York itself was great," he said with a crooked smile. "And the trip down was enlightening."

Debra raised an eyebrow. "Oh, really? How so?"

Eli inhaled deeply then let out a long exhale. "Well, Jules told me the best thing I've ever heard in my life, followed by the most awful thing." He fixed his gaze straight ahead.

"What's going on, Eli?"

Eli couldn't get the words out. The sound that came out was the sound he'd been suppressing for four whole days and nights. It was an angry, violent cry that brought his dad in from the other room to witness his son fall apart.

"He raped her and tried to kill her, Mama...but she's strong and she lived, but she was hurt so bad...so bad," he sobbed into his mother's lap.

"Slow down, Eli. What are you talking about?" Sam King asked. Eli cried for another minute. "Talk to us please, Eli," he pleaded, wrinkles creasing his forehead on an otherwise smooth face.

Eli sat up and placed the heel of each hand beneath each eyebrow, but tears still rolled uncontrollably down his face. He had to start talking before he started weeping again.

"When Jules was seventeen, she was drugged, raped, and beaten. He tried to kill her."

Debra and Sam exchanged pained glances.

"He hurt her so bad," he cried.

"Was she taken to Mass General?" Sam asked. "Was a police report filed?"

"I believe yes, to both your questions," Eli said, wiping his tear-streaked face.

"Hold on. I'll be back shortly." Sam asked Eli for a specific timeframe before he picked up his cell phone and walked into his study. Fifteen minutes later, he emerged with his tablet and sat down on the couch.

"I was able to obtain the police report online since it's public record. Jules's name is nowhere in the report, but a seventeen-year-old female was raped at a frat house on the Boston College campus. And you know the law—as a doctor,

I can't violate her medical confidentiality—but I can confirm that Jules told you the truth. Her injuries were severe and quite extensive."

"Start from the beginning and tell us what you know," Debra encouraged her son.

Eli cleared his throat and swiped at the tears that seemed to keep falling. "We've spent a fair amount of time together since she's been back, but she kept telling me she didn't want to go downtown. I couldn't figure it out, but I knew something was wrong, and she didn't want to talk about it. I'd tried to coax it out of her a few times, but she was having none of it. So when we got in the car for the four-hour drive to New York, she started talking to me. First, she told me she loved me…and I told her the same," Eli smiled.

"That's wonderful, honey!" Debra couldn't get it out fast enough.

"How long has this been going on between you two?" Sam asked.

"Almost a month now. Then we went back and forth on that for a little while, and then she repeated a previous warning: she told me that the information I wanted to know was something I couldn't 'unknow.' And she was exactly right.

"Jules said she was avoiding a specific person who lived and worked downtown because he's the one who hurt her— only I didn't know she'd been hurt. She wouldn't say his name. All she'd say was that we know him. She told me he took her out two weeks before her senior year of high school started, right before his senior year at Dartmouth. He tried to rape her that night, but she got out of the car, and he got mad and threw her purse out at her and left her. She called her best friend to come and get her."

"Did she tell her parents?" Sam asked.

"She said they weren't home when she got there, and she felt like it was her fault, so she didn't say anything. Then he tried again the week before her winter break. He cornered her in the high-school library basement while she was working on a project. She was only able to get away from him because the library director was getting off the elevator, and the guy was distracted long enough for her to escape. The weekend after that, she went to a cookout that Chris was having at his frat house. That's where it happened. The guy gave her a drink spiked with ketamine. Then he tied her to a bed, put on a condom, and preceded to destroy her," he said, as tears streamed down his face.

"And do you know what Jules is worried about?" Eli asked. Sam and Debra looked at each other then back to Eli. "She's worried that the two of you won't want us to be together because she can't have babies. And she can't have babies because Denny Griffin took that away from her," he cried.

"She really said that?" Debra asked. "This thing between the two of you sounds pretty serious."

Eli nodded. "I want to marry her."

"Oh, Eli." Debra beamed through tear-filled eyes.

"That's wonderful, son," Sam said, placing a hand on Eli's shoulder. "Does she know?"

"No, Pop! We've only been dating for like a month."

"Well, it's obvious she knows how she feels about you, so she made a hard yet mature decision to tell you about this," Debra acknowledged.

"When we got to her friend's apartment in the city, she finished telling me this grim truth. She told me she wasn't able to have children. Even though I told her I loved her a few hours before this, she looked at me and told me she wanted me to weigh both sides of this issue thoroughly before I made any decisions about how to proceed with our relationship. She told me I had to be able to live with the fact that we can't have biological children together. And she didn't think you guys would be okay with it because, in her words, it'd be a waste of good genetics."

"What did you say, son?" Sam asked.

"I told her that was crazy, and I wouldn't entertain any possibility that didn't have us together. Jules begged me to reconsider, but I couldn't, and I know she relented for her own sanity. I just can't *not* be with her. I told her we'd deal with all of it together."

"We know you love her, son. At least I've known since the night of Jules's junior prom. You had her date so scared—Thomas was impressed and appreciative," Sam said with a laugh.

Eli looked up at his dad. "What are you talking about?"

"Don't you remember? You were home on spring break. It was the weekend before you went back to school, and you were in a terrible mood because that kid you didn't like was her date." Sam was sure it would click for his marvelously intelligent son.

Eli nodded. "That's right…Drew O'Neill. I went to fix Mr. D's laptop, and that's when I ran into him. I remember now. Wow, you knew that long ago?"

"I did. You're my son. I'm proud to say I made you, raised you, and know you. And I knew you were in love with Juliana Dempsey then, just like I know it now."

"You said earlier that it was Denny Griffin. How do you know that?" Debra asked Eli.

"Jules had no recollection of what actually had happened for more than a year. She was in therapy, explaining to someone what happened, and she said his name. That's when it clicked for her. He was the same guy who'd tried to rape her twice before."

"Was there any proof?" Debra continued.

"Not really, and as she put it, the only DNA on her was her own. But he beat and raped her so badly that several of her internal organs were damaged." The tears started to flow again. "I'm really sorry to come over here and unload all this on you, but I think I was in shock when she told me, and I've been holding it in ever since."

"Don't you dare apologize," Sam said, gently grabbing Eli by the shoulder. "We're your parents. And I think I speak for both of us when I say of course you have our blessing to marry Juliana." Debra nodded in agreement.

"She goes by 'Jules' now, Pop." Eli smiled a little through his tears. "What are your thoughts about her not being Jewish?"

"Your mom wasn't Jewish," Sam said. "She converted because she wanted to."

"And because your grandmother nearly insisted. But yes, I wanted to. Of course we'd love it if she decided to convert, but that's totally her decision," Debra said, holding her son's hand.

"Thanks, because your blessing means the world to me, and I didn't even know how much it means to her."

"Just make sure you ask Tommy before you propose; she's his only daughter."

"Your dad's right," Debra said.

"Come on." Eli looked at them with first sign of relief on his face. "You guys raised me better than that. Of course I'm going to ask Mr. D."

When Jules got home, it was late afternoon. Lovey was sitting on the couch, watching TV and knitting something she'd just started.

"Hey, Lovey, where are Ma and Dad?"

"There was a function at church this afternoon," she answered.

"You didn't want to go?"

"No, I passed. I've been to enough church functions, and there's a *Die Hard* marathon on right now. I really like that Bruce Willis."

"Me too," Jules said with a smile as she sat down beside her grandmother. "They left you here alone?"

"I'm not an invalid." Lovey cut her eyes behind her glasses. Her gray hair was swept up off her face in a twist. "Besides, I knew you were coming home. I sorta thought Eli would be with you, though."

"I left him at his place. I needed some room to breathe."

"How was your trip?"

"Enlightening and exhausting." She paused for a long moment. "I told Eli what happened…you know, when I was seventeen."

"And?"

"And…you were exactly right," Jules admitted.

"Was I now? About what?" Lovey asked knowingly.

"He told me I was his first love. Then I had to tell him about being raped," Jules said with a sigh.

"He's loved you for a while now, huh? I knew I sensed a longing there."

"Am I crazy, Lovey? I just don't know what to do."

"The only thing you have to do is love him, honey."

"I do love him, but the situation is so fragile and complicated."

Lovey put down her knitting and placed a hand on her granddaughter's knee. "You just handle it together. That's what being in a relationship is: teamwork, compromise, communication, the company of your best friend, and fantastic lovemaking," Lovey said, her hazel eyes staring straight at Jules.

"That's what Eli said. That first part anyway. He wouldn't even weigh both sides of the situation because he said if he agreed to that then it implied a possible outcome would be us not being together and that wasn't a possibility." Jules looked like she was going to cry as she sank into the couch beside Lovey.

"Can I ask what's got you making that face?"

"I'm afraid I won't be enough for him," she said, her voice shaking.

"Oh, honey, it seems to me he can't get enough of you. The first day you went to the office, he was over here that night. I think dinner was next. Then, if I remember correctly, he came to kiss you at the pool. You went out to the bar with him then spent the night at his place. After that, the two of you had dinner at his apartment. And now you just spent four days together in New York. I'm sure you see my point."

Jules inhaled a deep breath. "I do."

"And you, my sweet granddaughter, are the first person I can think of who deserves something wonderful. As far as I'm concerned, Eli is your wonderful." She smiled. "What do you say we go upstairs and turn on the vaporizer?"

"After you, Lovey."

Chapter 12

*E*li had been working in his office for the better part of the morning. He was so engrossed in his work that it took him a moment to notice Thomas Dempsey sitting in front of him. Mr. D had a few questions about certain stipulations in a couple of contracts Eli had drawn up. They discussed his questions at length, and Eli made notes regarding what he needed to change in several clauses.

"Sir, if we're finished talking about the contracts, I have something else I need to speak with you about," Eli said, sounding very businesslike.

"Sure, Eli. What is it?" Thomas asked.

"Sir, you know I went with Jules to New York this past weekend, right?"

Thomas nodded. "I do, yes."

"Well…sir…I'm in love with your amazing daughter, whom I've been friends with for most of my life. I want to ask her to marry me, but since she's your only daughter, I wanted to ask your permission first. I thought about asking you and Mama D together, but I just couldn't wait."

"Have you bought her a ring yet?" Thomas asked trying, to conceal his smile and delight.

"I bought it yesterday, when I left my parents' house," Eli said, taking the small black-velvet box out of his inside breast pocket. He placed the box on the edge of his desk, in front of Thomas, who picked it up and opened it. "Her hands are so small…I didn't want to get something that would look gaudy on her finger."

Thomas examined the tasteful three-stone diamond ring, which measured slightly more than a carat. The center stone was a half-carat, emerald-cut diamond, and the two emerald-cut diamonds on either side of it were a third of a carat each. The diamonds were set in platinum.

"You took a big gamble that I would say yes, Eli." Thomas looked at him seriously. "There are issues that…complicate this situation," he added hesitantly.

"I know what happened to Jules when she was a teenager—she told me," Eli said, looking him directly in the eyes. "She told me all of it. I know she can't have children too."

"Did you tell your parents about all of this? Do they know she can't have children and that you want to marry her?" Thomas scratched his strong, shaved chin.

Eli nodded. "Of course."

"And what did they say?"

"They gave us their blessing and made sure I knew to ask you first."

"Eli…I already love you like you're one of my own, but she's my baby. And I know you're in love with her." He smiled. "I can tell by the ring…and especially if you're in…especially after what she told you."

"I'm in love with her, and I have been for a really long time."

"And you know she's going to move to New York after her grandmother eventually passes?"

"I do."

Thomas sighed. "What are we going to do about that, Eli? I'm not sure what I'd do here without you. Plus, what are we going to do about Jules's living arrangements? She's here to save me from spending my retirement on elder care for my mother."

"If it's okay with you, I thought we'd just proceed as we are now. On the nights she stays with me, she'll return for Lovey at seven the next morning, or whatever time you like. And if you wouldn't mind, when Jules needs to stay at your house, I could come too, and we could sleep in the family room like we used to when we were kids. So then you'd know there wasn't any funny business happening. That way we'd stay at your house some too. Fair?"

Thomas nodded.

"As for finding my replacement," Eli continued, "I was planning on crossing that bridge when I came to it. Truthfully, when I decided I wanted to propose, I hadn't thought that far ahead. But this morning I was in contact with the realtor Jules has been working with. There's a brownstone in foreclosure that she loves. It's in a great location, on West 67th and Columbus Avenue, and the X3 fits in the garage perfectly. I know foreclosures can take a while, so I wanted to see if there's been any interest in it."

"What if I say no?" Thomas was testing Eli's acumen.

Eli grinned; he knew what Thomas was up to. "You won't…because you know there isn't another man in the universe who'll love her and take care of her the way I will."

Thomas was quiet for a moment while he studied Eli's face. Eli continued to look directly at him. "I wasn't going to say no, but that's a damn good argument son." He smiled broadly then stood and reached out his hand, and Eli rose to meet him. "Few things would make me happier...but please stop by the house and show this beautiful ring to Helene. On second thought, would it be okay if I called her and asked her to come here? Your future Mrs. isn't scheduled to be here today. I wouldn't want to spoil the surprise if she were to catch you at the house." Thomas was always thinking ahead.

Eli smiled again. "I don't mind at all, but you two have to keep this to yourselves. This relationship is very new, and I don't want to freak Jules out. I want to date her for a little while before I propose, but I'd love to show the ring to Mama D."

"Very good. I'll order some lunch. That's sure to get my wife over here." Thomas chuckled at the door.

Thirty minutes later, Eli heard Helene talking to Philip, who was in the middle of telling her about the complete outfit of a client who'd been in there earlier in the week.

"Her shoes alone had to cost at least fifteen hundred but probably closer to two thousand. It's absurd! But they were unmistakable. Christian Louboutins...gorgeous."

"And speaking of gorgeous," Eli said, walking up to Helene, "how are you, Mama D?"

"Oh, Eli, it's always nice to see you," Helene said with a smile.

"Hi, sweetheart. I thought I heard you." Thomas came out of his office. "Philip, there's enough lunch here, if you'd like to eat with us—"

"Thank you for the invitation, sir, but my husband and I are having lunch with his brother. My brother-in-law is at the restaurant, waiting on us now. Let me set up the conference room, and then I'll go." Philip started to get up.

"No, no. It's okay, Philip. You go ahead to lunch. See you in an hour…In fact take all the time you need," Thomas said.

"Yes, sir," Philip said, grabbing his messenger bag. "And I'll drop these by the municipal courthouse on my way," he said, as he headed out of the door, stuffing an armful of files into his bag.

"Thanks, Philip," Thomas called after him.

Thomas, Helene, and Eli walked into the conference room, where Greek salads, with grilled salmon atop, were waiting for them. They sat down as Helene was thanking her husband for the thoughtful lunch.

"As much as I love seeing you in the middle of my day for no reason at all, honey, I needed to get you here, and I knew this would do it," Thomas began.

"Why? What's going on?" Helene asked.

Eli placed the ring box in front of her on the table.

"Is that what I think it is?" Helene looked between Eli and her husband. She picked up the box and opened it. She let out a tame squeal and bounced her feet up and down.

"I haven't asked her yet, and I'm not going to for a while, so please don't say anything." Eli sounded like he was pleading.

"Oh Eli, we wouldn't dare," Helene nearly exclaimed.

"Thank you both. I knew I could count on your discretion."

It was late summer now, ten weeks or so after Eli had asked for Thomas Dempsey's permission to marry his daughter. To Helene's dismay, Jules still wasn't sporting that gorgeous engagement ring, but she was exclusively attached to the beautiful man who was going to give her that ring. So for the moment, it was enough for Helene.

Tonight was a busy night, but it was going to be a night very similar to the previous nights Eli and Jules had spent together since their trip to New York, in that they'd be together. And they'd spent most of their nights together since New York. Some nights Jules would go to Eli's when Helene got home and return the next morning around seven to make Lovey breakfast. Other nights Eli stayed with Jules at her parents' house. There was no lovemaking those nights. In fact, on those nights, just as Eli had suggested, they slept in the family room, like they used to do when they were kids. Most of those nights, they welcomed Lovey's company. They watched movies and talked. Eli got a glimpse of Jules through Lovey's eyes.

However, tonight a fundraiser for the Dempsey campaign was taking place. The Friday-night event was being held in the ballroom of a swanky hotel in downtown Boston.

At this point in the evening, they were about halfway through a silent auction, the proceeds of which would go to Thomas's reelection campaign. Everyone there was one of his constituents: small-business owners, fellow lawyers, nurses, police officers, doctors, teachers, et cetera. Tonight was also an amazing opportunity—for anyone who was so inclined—to network with Boston's who's who.

Jules was wearing an empire, halter, floor-length chiffon evening dress. The top was a pale pink to right below her breasts, and then the dress was a dark chocolate from right below her breasts to the floor. She was wearing those high-heeled Prada sandals too. Contrary to the slight angst she felt on the inside—there was a good chance Denny Griffin would attend this shindig—Jules dazzled on the outside. Eli couldn't stop looking at her. He was supposed to be working the room, as was she. Jules wasn't really working the room per se—it was more like she was making small talk with the people who were in her vicinity…and there were lots of people in her vicinity.

Eli had been busy; people loved to talk to him. Even though he'd been "working" all night, he'd kept Jules in his sight for more than an hour. Eli saw that Jules had made her way to the edge of the room, near the doors that led to the veranda, as the emcee began to wind down announcing the winners of the silent auction. That's when he saw *him.* Eli saw Denny Griffin…and Denny was watching Jules. He was standing at the bar, and his eyes were plastered to her. The blonde beside him talked mindlessly while he just watched… Jules. It took every ounce of Eli's strength to contain his fury and anger.

Jules walked through the open doors to the veranda. The breeze was warm but also cooling as it brushed over her skin. Denny made his move toward Jules, and so did Eli. Eli had been closer to her the whole time. He walked out behind her, in full view of Denny, slid his arms around her waist from behind, and kissed the side of her neck. The move was completely possessive. When Eli turned toward the open doors, he didn't see that Denny had stopped on the other side of the door and was talking to a small group of people. In fact Eli didn't see Denny at all. He didn't tell Jules that Denny was there because he didn't want to startle her. He planned to try to get them out of there without her knowing.

"Hey, beautiful, you want to sneak out of here and go back to my place?"

Jules flashed him a sly smile. "You wouldn't get in trouble with your boss, would you?"

"No way...Besides, the guy your dad's running against has pending charges described as 'various types of fraud,' so I'm not incredibly worried about his losing."

"Then, yes, let's leave please."

"Let me find your dad and tell him we're leaving," Eli said, walking beside her on her left, blocking her from where he thought Denny would be standing. He looked around but didn't see Denny anywhere in the immediate vicinity, so he relaxed a little.

"I need get my purse from coat check."

"Wait until after we tell your dad." Eli was distracted as he spoke; he was looking for Denny. Thomas and Helene were speaking to another couple when Eli and Jules found them.

"Hey Daddy, would you mind if we go?"

"No, I suppose it's fine. The function is winding down."

"Jules, before you go, would you come with me to say good-bye to Violet? She and Ervin are getting ready to leave." Helene walked her daughter toward Violet as she talked. Eli didn't want to just yell out his warning that Denny was there, so he tried to be extra vigilant and still pay attention as Thomas Dempsey talked to him.

Violet was one of Helene's oldest friends. She was short, with shoulder length-blond hair. The deep lines in her face were due to years of smoking. It was Violet's daughter, Bethany, who had picked up Jules when Denny had kicked her out of the car on their date. Jules and Bethany had been good friends in high school.

"Great turnout tonight," Ervin said, as he put his champagne glass on the tray of a passing waiter.

"Yes, it was. Thank you both so much for coming," Helene told them both.

"Jules, that dress is fabulous," Violet complimented her.

"Thanks, Violet. I was just glad I had something appropriate to wear tonight." Jules smiled. "How's Bethany doing?"

"She's doing great. She married a man in the navy. They're living in Gaeta, Italy, and she's teaching American kids on base."

"That's terrific. Can I get her e-mail address from you?"

"Sure, I'll send it to your mom." Violet looked at her husband.

"Honey, I'm going to the ladies' room while you get the car. Helene?"

"You're reading my mind, Vi. Jules?"

"No, Ma, I'm okay. I'm going to get my purse." She kissed her mother on both cheeks. "Good night, Ma. Good night, Violet," she said in Violet's direction.

As Jules walked back toward the coat check to retrieve her purse, she heard her name, "Juliana." She found it strange because most people tonight hadn't called her by her given name. When she turned to her left, she saw Denny Griffin standing there. Upon sight of the nuclear slime, her deepest fears manifested. Her ears were buzzing, and her heart slammed against her chest. She didn't know if she was going to throw up or pass out and hit the floor. She wished hell would open up right then and there and swallow him whole.

Only moments after she heard her name, and had yet to respond, Eli walked up right behind her and whispered in her ear, "I got you," and possessed her with the very same move from outside. This time he kissed her on the lips.

"Juliana," Denny said again. This time he was in her personal space. Jules just glared at him. When she didn't answer, he said, "It's me, Denny."

"Who?" She looked at him with a dumbfounded expression.

"Denny Griffin," he said, looking as if he expected her to remember him fondly and embrace him.

"Right. Nice to meet you, Denny Griffin," she said, walking away.

"Nice to meet me? What the hell does that mean? She knows me, man. If you want, I'll tell you how I tightened that little ass up," he said to Eli.

"Shithead—" Eli began.

"Oh, my bad, man. You hitting that?" was all Denny got out before Eli walked away from him to get Jules and go.

Jules had just gotten her purse and was headed for the entrance to the hotel with Eli on her heels. She was almost running in those Prada heels and that fabulous dress. In her mind, she couldn't get away fast enough. The tears were coming, and she had to get away from where *he* was. Eli gave the valet his ticket then wrapped his hand around her biceps and pulled her to him.

"I got you, sweetheart. Calm down. Everything's okay. You didn't fall or cry. You're okay. Look at me," he pleaded. Those green eyes he adored peered up at him, filled to the brim with tears.

"Do you have any green at my house?" he asked, and Jules nodded.

The valet pulled up with Eli's car while she was still circled in his embrace. Eli opened the passenger-side door and helped Jules in, closed the door, and went around to his side. The Land Rover roared to life; within minutes they were at his front door, where she was shaking in his arms. Jules had held it all in during the ride over and had yet to say a word, but tears were now freely flowing down her face. Eli got her to the couch in the den.

"Jules, talk to me." She didn't say a word. "Jules, baby, please." The tremble in his voice was audible.

"Okay, what do you want to talk about?"

Shit, Eli thought, *she's in shock.* "Jules, do you know what happened about twenty minutes ago?" His eyes met her blank stare. *No, no, no.* Silently, Jules got up from where she sat beside him and walked upstairs to his bedroom. Eli stood and followed her. She unhooked the clasp at the nape of her neck that held her dress together. Then she stepped out of her dress, threw it over the chair in the corner, and crawled into Eli's bed.

"About twenty minutes ago…" Eli encouraged her.

"I saw him," she said, looking up at Eli. "And I'm okay. Thank you."

Thank God she was listening. "Oh, baby, I'm so sorry that I didn't get to you before he saw you."

"Elijah King, don't you dare apologize to me. You kept me upright and got me away from him. Thank you." The tears continued their descent down her face.

"I love you, beautiful. I promise you with everything I have that I'll never let anyone hurt you, especially *him.* Please don't cry. I know it's selfish to ask that, but my heart can't take it, baby." The tears were quickly giving way to the sobs she'd been holding in. Folding herself into a ball on Eli's bed, she couldn't stop the sobs from racking her body. Eli put his arms around her and held on until the sobbing and shaking finally stopped. It got a little worse before it got better, but he continued to hold her, trying his best to soothe her.

When Jules looked up, she saw Eli's eyes were red and puffy, and his face was tear streaked. Jules frantically wiped his face. She looked so confused.

"What's wrong, Eli? I don't think I've ever seen you cry."

"What can I say? You're my Achilles' heel…and you have my heart. When you hurt, my heart hurts." He kissed her forehead, and she exhaled, seemingly calmer than she'd been in the last half hour.

"Where's your green, baby?" he asked.

"In your nightstand by your condoms."

"We won't be needing these anymore," Eli said, as he tossed the condoms onto a shelf and handed her the bud. Jules hurriedly broke the bud and packed it into her glass bowl. She lit, inhaled, and held it in.

"What are you going to do with those?" she asked, pointing to the condoms. She passed him the bowl after she'd hit it a few times.

"Probably give them to one of the guys I play pickup games with. Inevitably one of them will need them. I know how much you hate waste." He exhaled a puff of smoke.

"I do." She smiled a little. "Thank you for being with me, Eli," she whispered. She looked so tired and defeated, even after she should have been good and high. Eli couldn't stand it.

"I wouldn't be anywhere else." He gently stroked the nape of her neck. "Hey, baby, sit tight. I'll be right back," he said, getting up from the bed.

"Eli…"

"I'm not leaving, love." He walked into his closet and, a few moments later, walked out wearing a white T-shirt and athletic shorts. He also held that small box in his hand.

He crawled back into bed. Jules looked so sad—so much so that he thought he might lose it all over again. This beautiful woman, *his* beautiful woman, was much stronger than she realized. She had stared evil in the eyes and won—thrown him off his game even. Despite her fear, Jules had been quick on her feet. Right now, however, she was about to go over the edge, and he didn't want to lose her.

"Baby, do you love me?" Eli asked.

"Yes, I do. You know I do…and I have for a really long time," Jules said, leaning into him.

"I love you too, Jules, with everything I am as a man. I love you. I wasn't going to do this tonight, but I just hate that you've been…distraught, and for whatever reason, I can't just let you be." He held out the little box. Jules looked at it and blinked up at Eli, her eyes wide and full of surprise. She sat straight up and took the box from his fingers.

"Jules Dempsey," Eli began, "would you do me the honor of being my wife?"

Jules thought about pinching herself. Was this for real? It had to be for real—she was holding a little box.

"Open it, beautiful," Eli encouraged her.

Her hands shook with anticipation. As she lifted the top of the box, her eyes were brimming, this time with happy tears. "Oh, Eli, it's beautiful," she whispered. "I'd marry you even without a ring."

"So…does that mean you're saying yes?" Eli asked.

"Yes, but—" she started.

"No, buts, Jules. I'm not going to let you analyze your way out of this. I'm in love with you, woman, and I want you to be mine. You're mine, and I'm yours."

"There are so many things we have to figure out," she said.

"Like what? It doesn't matter. I promise it's nothing we can't handle together."

"I'm not Jewish for one, and what if it's not okay with your parents?" she began.

"Jules, let me explain to you how serious I am about marrying you. The Sunday we came home from New York, I went to my parents' house after you went home. That's where I had my meltdown, so to speak. My guts, my head, and my heart hurt all at once. Please don't be mad, but I gave my mom and dad a rough synopsis of what you told me. I'm sorry if you feel like I violated your privacy or betrayed your trust. I just felt like the explanation was something they couldn't argue with, and I told you, you're mine. Without hesitation or reservation, they gave me, us, their blessing. When I left them, I went and bought your ring. Then I asked your dad. That was two and a half months ago. As far as your not being Jewish, that doesn't matter. My mom wasn't Jewish when she met my dad. Convert, don't convert…I don't care. All I know is that we're going to get married and live happily ever after. You want to?" Eli looked at Jules with complete sincerity in his eyes.

She smiled. "I already said yes."

"You said, 'Yes, but,'" he countered.

"Yes, Elijah. I'll marry you." She laid her lips on his, and they kissed.

"Really?" Eli asked, pulling back.

She caressed his face. "Yes, really."

"Let's see how this baby fits." He took the ring out of the box and slid it on her finger.

"It fits perfectly," she cooed. "I can't believe you proposed to me."

"Why not?" He looked at her a little sideways. "You still don't believe I love you?"

"Let's just say this crystallized it for me," she said with a shy smile. "Besides, it's *my* flaws that scare me…not yours. You already said you'd never hurt me."

"I swear to you, you're my heart—"

"I believe you, Eli. I have ever since you first told me you loved me. I just…have to acknowledge it, because previously it wasn't 'normal' for Eli King to be in love with me."

"Well, get used to it, beautiful, because that's the norm from here on out. You don't ever have to wonder if I love you. The caveman part of my brain is in overdrive when it comes to you. All you have to do is ask, and my answer will always be the same: I love you, Jules."

⌘⌘

The next morning, Eli and Jules invited their parents to brunch to deliver the good news. Everyone was ecstatic; Helene decided Eli should be the one to tell Aaron and Chris. After all these years, these two families finally would be…family.

$\mathcal{A}$fter brunch, Eli and Jules were going back to Eli's to discuss some things and make plans. When they got back to his place, Jules went upstairs to the couch and turned on the television. He'd gotten her hooked on *House of Cards.*

Eli sat down beside her. "You want to talk about it?"

"What?"

"About how freaked out you are right now."

Jules shrugged. "I'm not freaked out." She wouldn't look at him.

"I'm calling bullshit, Jules. You haven't said two words since we left brunch. You have times where you're quiet, but they're rare." He smiled at her. "Please tell me what you're thinking. Tell me what you want."

Jules sighed. "I wasn't sure I'd ever get married. I never, ever thought I'd be marrying you. I just knew that after almost ten years you'd be married to some unbelievable beauty with a couple of beautiful children, but you're not—you're here with me. So that realization is sinking in, and it's weird, but I've never seen our parents happier."

"Whatever doubts you have running through your head that you're not telling me—stop it. I don't know why I didn't fulfill your version of my life: the fictional family, but I didn't…I'm here with you. I love you."

"Wow. Really?" She knitted brows together slightly. *How's he reading my mind? Get out of my brain, Elijah!*

"Yes, ma'am. I also have something for you from New York."

"What could that be? We were together the whole time. And that baklava would be too old and hard to eat now," she called after him, laughing.

"It's not the baklava." Eli handed her a folder a quarter of an inch thick.

When Jules opened it, she couldn't believe her eyes. She was looking at a picture of the brownstone on the top page of all the papers in the folder.

"What am I looking at, Eli?"

"I talked to Lorraine. I wanted her to know we're interested in the brownstone that's in foreclosure…if you want it."

"That's another thing…I can't stay here. I can't live in Boston. Oh, my God, you'll have to move. I hadn't even thought of that. You'll have to take the New York State Bar."

"I can start studying for the exam now. I passed one; I can pass another. It's not like we're moving tomorrow. Jules, baby, I just handed you the paperwork that puts in the bid for the brownstone if you okay it. Lorraine said it was better than the asking price, and the bank will accept the offer. I'll go anywhere you want, and I was hoping you'd want me to go to New York with you and move into that brownstone where the X3 fits perfectly in the garage."

"Eli, you…you bought me a house?"

"No, not yet, but all it will take is a phone call to start the paperwork…and as soon as we get married, it'll be our house, and we'll be buying it *together*."

"This is too much," she said, shaking her head.

"No, Jules, after being in love with you for almost twenty years, it's nowhere near enough. I'm just getting started. We're going to have a life together. I want you to think about what you want in terms of our wedding: where, when, how big or small. We have to plan this."

She eyeballed him. "Don't you think your ma and my ma will have every last detail of it planned out?"

"That's why I'm trying to discuss this with you. If we stay focused and have a plan, we can keep them from going crazy with this," he explained.

"You, sir, still have to tell Chris and Aaron," she said with a smile.

Eli grinned. "Don't change the subject, my future Mrs. King."

"What do you want for the wedding, Eli? You're part of this process too." She laid her head on his shoulder.

"I want to marry you, so whatever you want, I want."

"That can't be it. Do you want to wear a suit or a tux? Do you prefer roses, tulips, or calla lilies? What colors do you like or hate? Oh, my God, we're planning a wedding!"

"*Our* wedding," he corrected.

"Yes, even more so. We're planning *our* wedding." Jules smiled and looked at her ring yet again. It was her tangible reminder that this was actually happening. Eli loved her as much as she loved him. They were getting married, and they were going to spend the rest of their lives together.

"I'd prefer a suit. Calla lilies are nice, and I'd prefer a small wedding, if that's okay. This is for you and me. I know our parents are going to feel obligated to invite some people, but this is for us. We could do a destination wedding. Then maybe just our families and a few close friends would come, because I know you don't want to get married in Boston."

"No, you're right. I don't. Maybe somewhere warm. What about Jamaica?"

Eli raised an eyebrow. "Are you marrying me in a bikini?"

"No, silly. We could have a simple ceremony, take some gorgeous pictures, eat some delicious food, and party the night away with people we love and who love us."

"That sounds perfect, and we could spend the next week to ten days there for our honeymoon." Eli was beaming. "The last time I looked into going there, I found private villas that aren't at a resort."

"You don't care about not getting married in a temple?"

"Not really. I'm sure my rabbi would come marry us on a white sandy beach if we bought him and his wife a ticket. Three days and a two nights seem fair?"

"I think so." Jules nodded. "Leslie and Jackie will come for sure," she thought aloud. "Okay, now you have to call my brothers."

"Done," Eli said, picking up his cell phone.

"Calling Chris first?"

"Yep, but don't look so worried. I'm not," Eli said, confident that his friend wouldn't have a problem with this. Eli put the phone to his ear; it rang a few times before Chris answered. Jules got up and walked into the kitchen in search of ice cream. She wasn't so sure Chris would agree so easily.

"Hello," came Chris's voice through the earpiece.

"Hey, Chris," Eli started.

"Eli, hey, man. How's it going? Is everything all right?"

"Oh, yeah, everything's fine. Do you have minute? We have a few things to talk about."

"Perfect timing, Eli. We just got the kids down. What's up?"

"We've been friends for most of our lives, and I figured I owed you this phone call."

"What's this about, Eli?"

"Jules and I have been dating since she came back to Boston at the beginning of the summer," Eli said matter-of-factly.

"Is that so? I never even knew you were interested in her." Chris paused. "Jules? Really?"

"Yes, really. But it goes a little further than that. I proposed Friday night."

"You proposed what?" Chris asked, either missing the point entirely or determined to make Eli explain himself.

"Marriage. I asked her to marry me."

"You proposed? To my sister?" Chris sounded shocked. "Are you serious?"

"Completely serious. I never told you, but…she was my first love."

"Your first love? Is this some kind of practical joke? You never even dated her. How can that be?" Chris was sounding more and more confused.

"Like I said, I'm completely serious. I didn't have to date to her to be in love with her," Eli stated.

"How come you never said anything?"

"I knew how you and Aaron felt about guys who liked her, so I wouldn't have ever said anything back then. It wouldn't have worked out then anyway, but we're adults now, and I'm in love with her. I just needed you to know that."

"Wow, Eli, I never would've guessed. But if my little sister makes you happy, so be it. Now I'm going to have to give you my 'big brother' speech."

"You want to do this now? 'Cuz I'd rather do it face-to-face. I'm totally down with listening to you and adhering to your expectations since you're Jules's big brother, but does it have to be right this second? And should I wait until before or after your 'big brother' speech to ask you to be my best man?"

"Are you serious, Eli?" Chris asked.

"Of course. I can't think of anyone who fits the description better. Besides, we're family now."

"As if we weren't before," Chris shot back.

"Touché, brother."

"When is this shindig supposed to take place? Do my parents and Aaron know yet?" Chris asked.

"My parents and your parents know—and they're thrilled. As far as I know, we're planning for late March or sometime in April. And no, Aaron doesn't know yet, but I'm calling him next."

"Give him another hour or so before you call. If not, call him tomorrow. His daughter does lots of extracurricular stuff. She dances, plays soccer, and does karate. I don't even think they're home yet. Then they do dinner, followed by homework and a bath before bed."

"Thanks, man, and I'm looking forward to seeing you."

"Yeah, man. See you soon. And congrats, brother-in-law!" Chris said before hanging up.

"Hey, baby. C'mere," Eli hollered from the couch.

Jules walked upstairs into the den, carrying a half-eaten pint of Häagen-Dazs pineapple-coconut ice cream. "How'd it go, counselor?"

"It's all good. Chris is going to give me his 'big brother' speech the next time we see each other, but that's okay."

"Really? You're going to let Chris have a 'big brother' talk with you?"

"Jules, he'll always be my best friend, and he'll always your big brother, so I have no issue with him saying whatever he needs to say. I'm marrying his baby sister, and I'm sure he just wants to make sure I'm going to do right by you and take care of you completely," he said looking directly at her. "I also asked him to be my best man."

"You *did?* What did he say?"

Eli smiled. "He said yes, love. What did you think he'd say?"

Jules shrugged. "I never actually thought about it."

"What about you? Who are you going to ask to be your maid of honor?"

"I thought I'd ask Sadie, Aaron's wife. Chris's wife, Morgan, can be a little reserved and probably won't want to be in the spotlight."

"Sounds good," Eli said. "Okay, I'm going to check the earliest availability for those private villas online now. Once we know which dates are available, we can proceed from there as far as plane tickets are concerned, and I can make a couple of calls on Monday. At least if we do it in the early part of the year, it won't interfere with the congressional campaign we'll be in the middle of," he said, walking toward the counter, where his laptop sat. When he returned to the couch, Jules wrapped her arms around his waist and kissed the spot where her lips landed on his back, just as he began to type in the words for his search.

"Jules," he said breathlessly, "my brain ceases to function when you touch me. I can't concentrate when you do that."

"That's exactly how it's felt to me for…well, forever, and you'd never even touched me. You just had to be in my air space—you simply exist and I'm totally distracted. Welcome to my world, counselor." She smiled coyly before she kissed that same spot on his back. This was her man; he loved her; and he was checking dates in Jamaica for their wedding.

"Let's go after Passover," Jules continued. "I'm sure your parents will want you here for that."

"You're so thoughtful, and you make a good point. What would you think about our anniversary being April twentieth, Miss Cannabis Connoisseur?"

"It'd be easy to remember." She smiled, and he laughed.

"Give me a few days to see what I can to do to make that happen, babe," he said, then kissed her on top of her head.

"I'm going to have to go shopping with my ma, and she'll want me to look like I belong on top of a wedding cake instead of eating it." She rolled her eyes. "Maybe I'll take your ma too. She can distract Helene."

"She'd love that. You have no idea how surprised and genuinely appreciative they were that you were concerned about them and how they'd feel about everything. They both really love you, you know?"

"That's so nice to hear," Jules said, "because I love them too. They made you, and although they didn't know it at the time, they made you just for me."

Chapter 14

About eight weeks later, it was nearing the middle of November, and it was one of the few evenings that Eli and Jules weren't together. Eli had gone out with his pickup-game friends, all of whom had noticed his absence. Dunleavy's was their favorite place to imbibe mostly beer, but a few cocktails too, and it was very a popular spot. Eli wasn't sure if he'd cross paths with Denny Griffin here again…but he hoped so. The guys had been at the bar for a few hours, and by now, it was only Eli and Patty. Several minutes later, Patty got his booty call and told Eli not to be a stranger before he left.

Denny Griffin took a seat at the bar less than ten minutes later. His dark-brown hair had been freshly cut, and it looked like he was wearing the same suit he'd worn to work.

Eli knew this couldn't have happened better if he'd planned it himself. Denny ordered his poison, Dewar's on ice, before he turned and spoke to Eli, who had sat down on the barstool next to him. Eli figured it wouldn't take many more drinks to get Denny's lips moving freely. He was wrong; Denny was nearly smashed already. Eli picked up his phone, which had been lying on the bar. He turned the microphone all the way up, hit "record," and turned his phone facedown.

"Eli King, I seem to keep running into you lately," Denny said.

"We do seem to be encountering each other frequently." Eli nodded as he placed his beer to his lips.

"Where's Juliana tonight? And what the fuck was up with her at her dad's fundraiser? She acted like she'd never met me." Denny seemed perturbed.

"I didn't know you two knew each other. You're a little older than I am, so it wasn't like you were in school with her."

Denny grinned. "Dude, that girl chased me around for years."

Lie.

"I just had to wait until she turned seventeen before I fucked her," Denny said before he sipped his Scotch. Eli glared at him. Denny was in bragging mode, because he had yet to ask about the relationship between Jules and Eli.

"So you and her were a thing?" Eli was asking leading questions.

"Ah, no, nothing like that. I'd just see her sometimes when I came home from college. She tried to act shy and played hard to get, but I came home on Christmas break one year, and we ended up at a party together."

Another lie. Eli didn't say anything at this point.

"Got a couple of drinks in that girl," Denny slurred, "and let's just say she couldn't get enough. And she liked it rough too."

The lies keep coming. Eli sipped his beer as Denny took another swig of his Scotch.

"Sorry if I ruined her for you, dude." Denny chuckled. "What's up with you two anyway?"

"We've gone out a few times," Eli said, trying to sound vague.

Denny shook his head. "I didn't even know she was in town, and you beat me to her."

"If you had her, why didn't you keep her?" Eli wasn't letting this go. This shit stain had tried, and failed, to ruin Jules, and had all but admitted it. Eli was praying that his phone was catching all this and that it was audible.

"She was a kid," Denny, said as he raised his hand to get the bartender's attention. "Besides, I was eyeball deep in pussy at Dartmouth."

"Yeah." Eli nodded as he stared vacantly in front of him.

"She told me once she was thinking of going to Emerson or UMass, so I thought she'd be around. I went by her house on what would've been her high school graduation, but her mom said she took early admission to the University of Miami. I hadn't seen her until I saw her here at the bar with you and then again at her dad's fundraiser. I can't believe she acted like she didn't know me. I took her virginity, for God's sake. I thought girls always remember their firsts," Denny said hatefully.

"I don't know, Den, but why don't I let you think on that for a while, 'cause I'm calling it a night," Eli said, picking up his phone and handing the bartender a fifty-dollar bill. "This is for my tab," he told him. "The rest is for you."

"Thanks, man," the bartender said.

Denny's protests were met with, "I got an early morning," and then Eli just walked away.

When Eli got into his car, he immediately started the engine because he needed to get away from there as soon as possible; Denny seemed to have that effect on people. Armed with the knowledge of what really had happened to Jules, Eli felt he completely understood her angst, from his secondhand experience of course. He hit "play" on his phone and listened to the entire conversation all the way home. A few parts of the conversation had competing noises in the background—people talking or glasses clanking on the bar—but the whole conversation was audible. He mentally high-fived himself.

It was after midnight when Eli's phone rang. It wasn't Jules, which disappointed him immensely. He tamped down his disappointment and answered the phone. It was Chris.

"Yo," Eli said. "Everything all right?"

"Yeah, Eli. Are you in bed with my sister?" Chris said, slurring a little.

"Are you drunk?"

"Not completely. It doesn't matter anyway—I'm sitting on my couch. So are you in bed with my sister?"

"Oh, no, no." Eli smiled. "Not tonight. Your grandma has some early-morning stuff to do, so Jules stayed home. I think Lovey wants to do some Christmas shopping."

"Good. I need to tell you something."

"What's that?"

"Like ten years ago, Jules got raped, and it was all my fault," Chris said sadly.

"Did you rape her?" Eli asked.

"Eww. No, man. That's fucking sick. What do you mean did I rape her? What the hell kinda thing is that to ask? I didn't rape Jules, and I—" Chris sounded pissed.

"Whoa! Whoa! Chris, hang on!" Eli interrupted him. "My point is that it wasn't your fault. You *didn't* rape her. It wasn't your fault. She doesn't think it's your fault. It wasn't your fault, man."

"It was my fault!" Chris almost shouted. "I was supposed to be watching her." He paused for a couple of seconds.

"Wait…how do you know about all this?" He sounded confused.

"You can't possibly think your sister was going to marry me and not tell me these things. She told me everything, and we're handling it together. I love her, and I can't imagine being without her now that I have her."

"That's so great, Eli," Chris said, sounding a little more relaxed.

"Hey, while I have you on the phone, let me ask you something," Eli said, transitioning the conversation.

"Shoot."

"Think back to that night and tell me what you remember," Eli probed.

"I was outside, manning the grill. There were so many people there. I gave Jules a burger and a beer and told her to go inside and watch the game. There were TVs hooked up everywhere, so I didn't go inside to watch, and like three hours later one of the pledges came running out to find me."

"Do you remember seeing Denny Griffin there?"

"Yeah, I do, but only because he told me he was bangin' this chick, Karen Anderson. She was fuckin' smokin' hot, and none of the guys I knew had ever owned up to fuckin' her, and we didn't know anyone who had. The keg was out by the grill, and the boos were inside. Denny came out and spoke to me while he was filling his cup. Karen came and got a beer from him. She winked and blew him a kiss when he handed her the beer, and then she walked away. He told me he had fucked her and proceeded to go into detail. Later, when I said something to her about knowing Denny, she had no idea who I was talking about." Chris was quiet for a minute. "Eli…

are you telling me Denny Griffin raped my sister?" he said through clenched teeth.

"Among other things, but yes," Eli replied.

Silence.

"Chris, you still there?"

"Jesus fucking Christ…Denny Griffin! I went over that night so many times in my head, but it never occurred to me once that it was him. Not once. I didn't even realize I remembered him being there until just now. Fuck, Eli. What now?"

"You can't breathe a word of this to anybody. Not your wife, your priest, or your parents. Don't even whisper it to your kids while they're sleeping. If there's some way we're able to take care of this, nobody can know we know. You got me?"

"Yeah."

"No 'yeah,' man. You got me? Seriously. I know that knowing this is hard, and I want to fucking kill him, slowly. But I'm figuring some things out. You just can't go pounding his face in. Just breathe, and don't say his name out loud; we don't speak his name. Got it? When I get this shit worked out, I'll let you know. Everything in due time. Have a little faith and patience. Understand?"

"I understand, Eli."

"Finish that drink and go to bed," Eli demanded.

"Ten-four."

The evidence Eli had gathered wasn't going to the police. Unfortunately the laws Eli had sworn to uphold had failed to protect and bring justice for the woman he loved. Denny never would spend a moment in prison for the heinous crime he had committed against Jules, even though he practically had confessed to it on tape. However, karma was about to surface, manifesting in a few unexpected ways.

◦◦◦ ◦◦◦

The next morning, Eli met his dad at the hospital before he started his rounds. Eli walked into Sam's office with a large coffee for him. Sam was pleasantly surprised and a little worried that he was looking at his son at six o'clock in the morning.

"'Morning, Pops, I got you a large black coffee."

"'Morning, Eli. To what do I owe this honor?"

"I'm really sorry to do this to you before you go on your rounds, but I ran into Denny Griffin last night."

Sam raised his eyebrows. "And what came of that?"

"I went to Dunleavy's with Patty and Brian and a couple of other guys. Once they left, I stayed to finish my beer, and Denny walked in five minutes later. He was pretty drunk, and he all but admitted what he did to Jules when she was a teenager. Except in his mind it was consensual, since she wasn't conscious and couldn't fight back or say no." Eli set his phone on his dad's desk. "I recorded the whole conversation," he said, bringing his eyes up to meet his dad's.

"Can I hear it?" Sam asked.

"Please," Eli responded, and hit "play." Sam listened intently with concern. Before the recording ended, he was looking up some information on his iPad. He seemed to have found what he was looking for because he began to make a list on a legal pad. Then he tore the top piece of paper off the pad and folded it in half. He still hadn't said anything yet.

"At six o'clock tonight, go to O'Malley's and ask for Mickey. I just handed you a list of the internal organs that were damaged when Jules was…hurt. Get the police report, let Mickey hear the recording, and give him the list." Sam King and Mickey O'Malley went way back, and Sam knew Mickey detested the idea of violence toward women.

"Why? What's he going to do?"

"He's in the business of comeuppance."

Eli just looked at his dad.

"Mickey's daughter was snatched from the school bus stop when she was seven. We looked for her for three days before she was found in an area that had been searched twice prior to that. She was a tough kid—she fought hard—but in the end she was just a little girl. I'd known the coroner for years, so he let me tell Mickey."

"I don't remember that."

"Good. I'm sorry I had to tell you about it now. I have no words to express what happens to a parent who loses a child. Trust me, you want to go see Mickey."

Chapter 15

*E*li did just as his father had instructed. He arrived at
O'Malley's promptly at six o'clock that night, opened
the door, and walked into a sparsely crowded room. Eli sat
down at the bar and asked the bartender if he could speak to
Mickey.

Mickey O'Malley was a forty-eight year-old full-blooded
Irish Bostonian. He stood a mere five foot eight, had a bald
head, thick hands and biceps, and a bad attitude, if there was
a need for one. Previously he'd been a lieutenant with the
Boston PD. Retirement had come early for Mickey when he'd
gotten shot once in the arm and once in the leg near his femo-
ral artery. He was the unspoken, unwritten rule for nightlife
at O'Malley's, as well as the surrounding area. He just kept
shit kosher, or as kosher as he could without getting caught
or locked up himself. Most of the time, people didn't go in
asking for Mickey.

He walked up and sat next to Eli at the bar. Mickey was
wearing a long-sleeve dress shirt with the first few buttons
undone, no tie, and jeans; he looked more casual than business, but he was all business. Eli swigged his Heineken, confident as ever.

"You asked to speak to me?" Mickey demanded.

"Yes, I did. I'm Eli King, Sam—"

"Sam King's your dad," Mickey interrupted him.

Eli nodded. "That's right."

"Come with me," Mickey said, as he got up and led Eli toward the back of the building, where they came to a set of stairs that led to the second floor. Eli followed him upstairs. On the second floor were two or three unoccupied offices. They walked into one, and Mickey waved his hand for Eli to sit down, while he remained standing, leaning against a desk.

"It's nice to meet you after all these years." Mickey softened his tone. "You're the lawyer, right?"

Eli nodded again. "That's right."

"Your dad has told me all about you, ever since you were a kid," Mickey said in a thick Boston accent. "Why don't you tell me about what's going on?"

"I have a police report here for you to look at. I also have a recording you should listen to," Eli began.

"You going to tell me what's going on?" Mickey asked again.

"When my fiancée, Jules, was a teenager, she was drugged, raped, beaten, and left for dead. It happened at her brother's fraternity party. The guy thought he killed her. Between the ketamine and the fact that there was so much internal damage, it's amazing she didn't die," Eli heard himself say, as Mickey looked at the file he gave him.

"There's something you should know. Her dad is US Congressman Thomas Dempsey, so I'm hoping for some discretion here."

Mickey nodded.

"The report says a hundred and twelve people were interviewed," Eli continued. "Several people saw her around, but nobody noticed when she wasn't around, and nobody saw where she went or knew what happened to her. Charges were never filed because Jules was drugged and couldn't identify the rapist at the time, but she knows now who did it." Eli handed Mickey the folded piece of paper from his wallet.

"Multiple lacerations to liver, kidneys, and spleen. Damage to the reproductive organs…" Mickey trailed off. "Christ," he huffed, "who did this to her?"

"A guy named Denny Griffin, and he all but admitted it to me in the recording that's on my phone."

"Let me hear it," Mickey said.

Eli hit "play" and placed his phone facedown on Mickey's desk. Mickey listened intently for a few minutes. "Jesus, she was a virgin." He shook his head. "Can I keep these?" Mickey held up the file folder containing the police report, as well as the list of Jules's injuries.

"Yes, those are yours," Eli said.

"Text me the file of that recording, will ya?"

"Sure. Give me your number, and I'll do it now," Eli offered. Mickey wrote his number down on a piece of paper.

"Don't save my number under my name," Mickey warned.

"No worries, but I think the file's too big to send. Let me download it to your computer. It'll just take a minute."

"Do that, and make it so it's easily accessible for me."

"Give me two minutes," Eli said.

"Has Denny seen her lately or have you noticed him around?"

"He knows she's back in Boston—she was in Miami for many years—and they…crossed paths at her father's last campaign fundraiser. I saw him, and then I didn't…and then I didn't get to her before he did," he said, sounding guilty.

"How'd that go down?"

"Jules is tough. She's got a quick wit, and she's great under pressure. As soon as he called her name, I walked up behind her and put my arm around her waist. He said his full name to her again, and she just blinked up at him all doe-eyed. Then she repeated his name back to him and said, "Nice to meet you," and walked away. That completely knocked him off his game, and he got pissed. As much I wanted to beat the shit out of him, I was more worried about her at the moment, so I went after her."

"Good man. That's what you do now. You concern yourself with *her,* and I'll concern myself with this. This isn't going to be a quick fix, and sensitive things like this take a lot of planning. Understand?"

"Yes, sir," Eli replied.

"When are you getting married?"

"We leave April eighteenth for Jamaica."

"Let's aim for somewhere around there. That way you'll both be out of town if there's any blowback. If I need anything, I'll call you."

Eli nodded.

"Good enough. Now get out of here," Mickey demanded.

When Eli walked out of O'Malley's at quarter to seven, he called Chris immediately to let him know what was up. He explained that he didn't know what was going to happen, but he didn't want to take any chances that Chris could mess it up. Even Chris knowing that it was Denny was one too many people, especially because Denny and his brother, Danny, had grown up with Chris and Eli.

"Will you keep me informed?" Chris asked.

"Yes, but no text messages," Eli directed. "Always call."

Chris agreed.

Denny was a couple of years older than them, but he'd been around, and Danny always had been around. This was betrayal—it was treason; it was just wrong and way too close. The problem now was that Chris had a face to put to the hurt that his sister and his family had endured.

Jules and Eli had spent the previous night apart, and Eli wasn't contemplating making it two. He called to see what the love of his life was doing at that moment. Helene's book club was there, and Jules all but begged Eli to come rescue her. He obliged. Mini quiches were in the oven, and Jules was pouring the red wine in the decanter when Eli rang the doorbell.

"I got it, Ma," Jules called out over her shoulder on her way to the door. "Good evening, counselor." She smiled as she stood on her tiptoes to kiss him. His hand found its favorite spot on her small, shelf-like booty.

"It is now, babe. Are you ready?"

"You have no idea. Let me tell Ma and say good night to Lovey."

Due to Eli's extravagant generosity, Jules never had to pack an overnight bag when she went to stay with Eli. All she had to take was herself. After their trip to New York, Eli had gone out and bought her a couple of pink toothbrushes and razors, all the skin and hair products her heart desired, and countless pairs of bras, panties, yoga pants, tank tops, and lightweight long-sleeve shirts. He even had bought her a few feminine hygiene products just to be on the safe side. She didn't just have a drawer either—he had moved a dresser from the upstairs bedroom downstairs, into his room, for her. He was serious.

The ride from Jules's house to his seemed treacherously long to him, but that was only because he wanted to strip her clothes off her and make her moan and whine while she bit down on her bottom lip. He couldn't keep his hands to himself; he just needed to touch her. She righted his world, and he needed that. He was still sort of reeling from his meeting with Mickey. When they walked into Eli's place, he made a beeline for the kitchen.

"I'm going to throw a pizza in the oven. Is that okay with you?" he asked, as he was preheating the oven.

"Sounds good, but I did graze some while I was helping Ma with the finger foods, so I'm not crazy hungry," she said, smiling at him.

Eli walked over to her and moved his big body close to hers. She tilted her head back to meet his eyes. He was trying to convey something; she just didn't know what. Eli ran his hand over her cheek as his fingers combed through her hair until his hand reached the back of her head and tilted her head back. Jules dragged air into her lungs. Their eyes were still locked.

"I know you don't want to get married here," Eli said, "but does that go for the whole state or just Boston in particular?"

Jules shrugged. "I guess I don't hate the whole state. Why do you ask?"

"Earlier today I caught myself thinking about when we were kids. A thought flashed into my brain. It was Chris, you, and me, and we were watching TV. Chris was giving you shit for trying to get him to change the channel to *The Simpsons* a few minutes early so we wouldn't miss the beginning."

"Okay. Where are you going with this?"

"We both love *The Simpsons,* and even though we have no idea what state they live in, we know they live in Springfield, so I want to take you to Springfield on Friday…and marry you," he said, as his lips planted light kisses on her neck. "We can spend the weekend there and come back Sunday afternoon."

"Eli, our moms are planning a whole thing in Jamaica. We don't need to get married so soon," Jules said.

"We do, Jules, for me. We do. It's the legality of it for me, babe. I need you to legally be my wife. We'll go to Jamaica for the ceremony and the celebration. Let's do this just for us. We don't have to tell anyone, and everyone will still be witnessing our union," Eli said, pleading his case.

Jules just stared at him.

"Say something, babe," he said.

"You're serious about this?" She looked up at him and studied his face.

"Absolutely. I wouldn't bring it up if I weren't completely serious. Please. Do this for me?"

"Well, when you ask like that…of course I will. Besides, I can't think of a thing on this planet I would deny you if it's within my power to do it. We don't have to stay the weekend, though. It's only like an hour and a half down the road, right?"

"If you're not busy with Lovey, I'd like to stay and have my wife all to myself for the first official weekend of our marriage."

"*Your wife…*I love the way that sounds," she cooed.

"No more than I do, beautiful, and it's taken far too long."

"Calm down, counselor. You just moved our wedding date from April twentieth to the day after tomorrow—a whole five months ahead of schedule."

"Jules, I'd have married you when I was eighteen."

"I was only fourteen when you turned eighteen. Your birthday is April fifth, and I didn't turn fifteen until December fifth. And it wasn't 1850—you couldn't have married me when I was fifteen."

Eli shrugged. "Legally, no, I couldn't have. But I loved you then, and I love you now."

Jules grinned. "It's just so crazy to me that we felt the same way but didn't know it."

"Oh, I knew you liked me. I heard your mom say it to somebody on the phone one time."

"You're kidding." Jules blushed.

"No, she told whoever it was that you were moping around because everyone was leaving for college, and your crush was going away to Brown."

Jules's face grew hot with embarrassment.

"I wanted to tell you that I felt the same way before I left, but you were my best friend's little sister, and I was leaving… so I didn't say anything. But from the moment I saw you sitting at your dad's desk when you first came back to Boston, I knew I was going to marry you."

"Your psychic powers are astonishing, Mr. King, and in one short day from now, you are indeed going to marry me." She smiled up at him. "You'll be my husband, and I'll be your wife."

"We'll have to be extra careful not to spill this to anyone," he said before he kissed her on her nose.

"That'll be a challenge for both of us. Hey, we don't even have wedding bands yet," she realized.

"Let's do that tomorrow. We can wear them the whole weekend then put them in the safe in my bedroom when we get home."

"I won't be free tomorrow until after the stores are closed."

"We don't have to be in Springfield by any certain time. I can have the license application couriered over to me tomorrow, so when we get to the hotel, we'll have the necessary paperwork to make this happen. Just you and me, babe. If you want, I can go get the bands myself."

"Well, you did an excellent job with my ring," Jules said. "But am I supposed to help you pick out the bands?"

"I don't think it matters, but we can look online if you really want to," he replied.

"Eli, you're not dying or going to prison or anything are you?"

"No. Why? What makes you ask me that?" Eli asked, confused.

Jules looked worried. "Promise?"

"Yes, I promise. What's got you worried?"

"I'm not really worried. I'm just surprised that you want to get married so badly," she said, trying not to sound critical.

"Oh, my God, woman! I'm in love with you—you're mine, and I'm not letting you get away from me. The ceremony is for everybody else. Friday is just for you and me."

"Eli, I'm not trying to get away from you. Of all people, you're the one person I'm running to," she reassured him.

"And that's why I'm marrying you the day after tomorrow. So you do whatever you need to do with Lovey, and I'll get our wedding bands. I'll go back to where I got your engagement ring. No worries, babe," he said, as he leaned down to kiss her.

The oven dinged to alert that it was preheated. Eli took the pizza from the freezer, unwrapped it, and put it in the oven.

"I have twenty-two minutes to make you scream my name as many times as possible," he said, nipping at her neck.

"You can't wait two whole nights until we're actually married?"

"Oh, no, Jules." Eli took her hand and placed it over his hardening erection. "You do this to me, baby."

"Let's go upstairs," she exhaled.

"The couch is closer," he nearly panted.

"The bed is bigger," she countered.

"Get past the couch, and I'll take you to bed…if I catch you," he said, and she took off running. She went straight out of the kitchen, took a left at the couch, and was about two steps past it when she noticed Eli was right on her heels. She took the steps two at a time until she reached the top. Eli grabbed her hand as she turned toward his room. Jules turned her body to him and pulled him to her.

The moment their lips met, he took off her clothes and backed her up to the king-size bed they shared. His hands blazed trails up and down her body while his tongue plunged in and out of her mouth.

"I want to do this every day," he growled.

"I'm going to hold you to that for at least three weeks of the month." She winked before she climbed onto the bed. Eli followed. Her short nails ran over his pecs and hardened nipples. He moaned into her kiss, and his cock instantly hardened. His strong fingers found her sensitive bud, and he rubbed it furiously.

"Ride me." He smiled at her as he situated himself on the edge of the bed.

"Gladly," she said, then lowered her moist opening over the head of his cock. Jules wrapped her arms around his neck, and Eli pulled her closer to him with the hand that wasn't stimulating her clit. She exhaled and pushed down onto his shaft a little farther before she slid back up. His mouth captured hers, and his hands wrapped around her ass as she quickened her pace, moving up and down rhythmically.

Jules tore her lips away and inhaled a much-needed breath. Eli took that opportunity to move his lips to her hard pink nipples. She felt the warmth of his breath before his wet tongue licked a few times, and then she felt a small sting as he nipped her nipple with his teeth. Right after the nip came his skilled tongue, licking away the pain, until she was screaming from the pleasure. When he sucked hard on her other nipple, she gasped as the tingling sensation went straight to her clit.

"I love you, Elijah," Jules said breathlessly. "I love it when you fuck me," she moaned. "I love it when you touch me," she barely managed before he took her other nipple in his mouth. "Oh, ah, ah, ah…shit! I'm coming," she said, trying to make her way to the top of his cock. He wrapped his arms around her waist and slammed her back down onto him. She moaned into his kiss while their hips ground together. Eli grabbed her ass and pulled her into him as he came inside her throbbing pussy.

"You blow my mind." He exhaled hard as he let the weight of his body fall back to the mattress. His semierect penis was still inside her, since she was still sitting atop his lap. He felt her lean to the side, so he gently pulled her down to his chest, where she rested her forehead and placed light kisses on his skin. Eli wrapped his arms around her body tightly and closed his eyes. He'd gotten her. The girl of his dreams. His love. And the most spectacular part was that she loved him back.

Chapter 16

It was a little after noon on Friday, and Eli couldn't get everything together fast enough. He must have touched the left side of his suit coat a hundred times or more. He felt the square box between his chest and his fingers. That particular little black box contained two matching wedding bands. His was a white-gold band with two slender eternity bands on both sides of the solid band. Jules's wedding ring consisted of four slender quarter-carat eternity bands that didn't connect in the middle; when paired with her engagement ring, the bands fit snuggly against the outer diamonds.

He had at least two hours before he could pick her up. Everything was packed, so he reviewed all the things he'd prepared. The marriage-license application accompanied the rings inside his suit-coat pocket. It had only been twenty minutes since he'd last looked at the clock. The waiting was agonizing. He picked up his cell phone and swiped his thumb across Jules's name. She answered sweetly.

"Baby, is your ma home yet?" Eli asked.

"She got home a few minutes ago. Why?"

"Is she leaving again? Does she have anything else to do?" he pressed.

"I'm not sure. What's up?" Jules tried not to sound worried.

"I'm just ready to go if you can leave anytime soon," he admitted.

"Let me check," she said, as she took the phone away from her ear. Her voice came back over the phone a few moments later. "Ma's going to church, but she's willing to take Lovey with her if you bring her a bottle of your choice of red."

"Done. What should I get her?"

"Go to the grocery store and get her Red Velvet by Cupcake. "It's less than fifteen dollars, and it's delicious."

"Okay. See you in thirty minutes or less."

"Bye, baby. Be safe. I love you," she said, smiling into the phone.

"I love you back," he said before hanging up.

Twenty-five minutes later, Eli arrived at the Dempsey house with a bottle of red wine for the woman he'd called "Mama D" for most of his life. Now their bags were packed and in the car, and Eli and Jules were strapped in and ready to go. There was snow on the ground; the sky was overcast; and they were both bundled up in coats, scarves, and gloves.

"Listen, wherever we're going in Springfield isn't going to move before we get there," Jules said. "Please don't drive like it's the autobahn. It's already snowed once today, and it's Massachusetts in the middle of November, it could snow again just because it's a day that ends in 'y.' And the last thing we need is a ticket."

"I'll drive the speed limit. Jeez." He shook his head.

"Where are we going anyway?"

"I told you…Springfield. We have reservations at a bed-and-breakfast," he said vaguely.

"You're not even going to tell me where we're going?" she asked, a little in disbelief.

"You know we're going to Springfield. Can't you just let me surprise you?"

Jules chuckled. "Okay, weirdo, are we going to eat once we get there?"

"Yes, baby, I have everything taken care of," he said while they drove down I-90.

"Well, can I at least see our rings?"

He smiled devilishly. "It's part of the surprise, babe."

"That's not fair," she almost whined. "You picked them out, so you know what they look like. I want to see them too." She batted her eyelashes at him.

"Please don't ever use the power you have over me for evil," he said, as he handed her the box that contained their wedding bands. Jules nearly blushed at his statement.

"Promise," she said, as she lightly clapped her hands before she took the box. When she opened it, her eyes widened then filled with tears as she looked at him. "Oh, Eli, they're beautiful," she said, her voice trembling a little.

"You like them?"

"You have impeccable taste, my love," she said before leaning over and kissing him once on the cheek and then under his ear.

"Okay, now you can't ask me any more questions. You'll see everything when we get there."

The journey straight down I-90 was completely unremarkable. Thankfully it hadn't snowed since earlier in the day. Eli hadn't told Jules, but he wanted to make it to Springfield before dark so they could get married at sunset.

When they arrived at Naomi's Inn, Jules couldn't believe her eyes. This quaint B&B was lightly dusted with snow and warmly decorated. Electric candles in the windows gave the house a lovely glow. It looked like a scene from an old-timey postcard.

"Eli, what a spectacular sight," she said, beaming.

He shrugged nonchalantly. "I didn't have anything to do with the snow or the decorations. I just found this place and made a few special arrangements."

"Like what?"

"Like…we'll be the only guests here until we leave Sunday afternoon," he said, leaning over the center console to kiss her. "And I went to college with a guy who's a judge in Concord, and he's going to be here at five to officiate."

"Eli…I had no idea. Wow!" She shook her head at him.

"What?"

"You always do things that make 'thank you' seem inadequate, but thank you. You're lavishly generous," she said, as she averted her gaze.

"What's wrong?" Eli asked.

"You know I'm not this high maintenance, right?"

"No, I don't think you're high maintenance," he shot back.

"I'm just so surprised…that's all." She tried not to sound defensive or ungrateful.

"I want to do these things for you. You have no idea how much enjoyment I get from the look of surprise on your face."

"Well, aren't you the romantic?"

"What can I say? You bring it out in me, beautiful."

"Let's go check in so I can freshen up before I become your missus," she said, opening her door.

Eli opened the trunk and took out the two heaviest bags and a wardrobe bag, and Jules grabbed her book bag and Eli's briefcase. Several minutes later, they were checked in and shown to their room. A few vases filled with calla lilies had been placed around the room. The table in the middle of the room had the largest vase, which sat off center, with personalized dinner and breakfast menus leaning against it. One of the owners had agreed that she'd happily make the food if Eli provided the ingredients.

The sage-colored room was simple and elegant. Two plush chairs and a walnut desk made up the seating area. Large coffee-bean-colored tiles provided a warm feel in the bathroom. A queen-size bed sat across from an antique daybed.

That daybed is going to be "smash tested," Jules thought with a grin. "Eli, you did all this?" she said, her eyes wide.

"Not physically, but I planned all of it for you…for us, for tonight."

He barely got the words out when Jules nearly jumped into his arms. He couldn't kiss her fast enough. Her hands were unbuttoning his shirt with speed and accuracy. Eli pulled off her sweater, unfastened her bra, and rolled one of her nipples between his finger and thumb. The pressure in his pinch was delicious; the sting from his bite kept her present; and his tongue lapped away any lingering pain she might have felt. He had her flat on her back on the bed, kissing, pinching, and licking her nipples and lips as she struggled to get her pants off. Eli sat up and grabbed the bottoms of the legs of her jeans then pulled them off the rest of the way.

Jules looked up at him with her piercing green eyes, which were glazed over like doughnuts due to the hormones, endorphins, adrenaline, and serotonin bathing her brain.

"I want to marry you, Eli, with a little bit of you inside me," she said, as she pulled him to her.

"You fucking drive me crazy, woman. And that, Ms. Dempsey, is another reason I want to marry you. You want me to claim you, as much as I want you to claim me," he said, as he pressed the head of his huge cock up to her moist entrance. "Guess we shouldn't shower till later then," he said, pushing in and filling her up.

Eli caught Jules's gasp in his mouth while their tongues tangled effortlessly. The chemistry between these two was overpowering, nearly flammable. His touch made her skin tingle, and though her pussy was filled to capacity, it throbbed and spasmed and clenched with pleasure; it was soaking fucking wet. It really was earth-shattering sex.

Afterward, as they lay there, sweat acting as the adhesive between their skin, Eli told her he had one more surprise for her—as if a secret wedding at a quaint B&B, with extravagant wedding rings, personalized menus for dinner and breakfast, and three orgasms within the hour weren't enough.

"What is it, Eli?"

He stood up and went to the closet, where he pulled out a wardrobe bag and unzipped it. "Clothes shopping for girls is something I've never done, but I was returning some dress shirts, and I saw this. Now if you hate it, please tell me, and of course you don't have to wear it. But if you like it, I'd like for you to wear it tonight and at least once in Jamaica."

Eli reached inside the bag and pulled out a floor-length, strapless, sweetheart chiffon dress. He really did know her well. The dress was iridescent pink. Pink was one of her favorite colors, and the dress he had picked out for her was gorgeous.

"Baby, wow…it's fabulous. You know, Elijah, if I didn't know you made love to me, and fucked me, like you were meant to and had two older sisters, I'd be worried about you. I've said before that you have impeccable taste, but you outdid yourself with this dress." She looked so happy and surprised.

"So you like it?" Eli asked, needing to hear it.

"I love it! I'll change into it after the ceremony in Jamaica."

"I'm looking forward to it. I'll also remember the first time you wore it."

Jules stood up and walked into the bathroom to wash her face and clean up any excess liquid between her legs. She fixed her makeup and put a few curls in her long hair. Eli pulled out his outfit to show her what he was wearing: a chocolate-brown suit with a soft-pink tie. Jules told him she didn't believe in luck, good or bad, so it didn't matter if they saw each other before they got married today. Today they could do things any way they wanted. They'd do it the traditional way for their parents, so her dad could give her away, but today was all about them.

It was a few minutes before five. The two of them walked down the stairs together, hand in hand, the way Eli wanted them to enter their union. The groom was pleased to find the honorable Judge Theodore Teller standing in the front room. Eli and Theodore entered a handshake that ended in hug.

Theodore stood about the same height as Eli, with short, receding brown hair and a well-kept beard. His deep-set eyes smiled as he saw Eli.

"Judge Theodore Teller, meet the future Mrs. Jules King," Eli said with a bright smile.

"Nice to meet you, Jules," Theodore said.

"Thanks so much for doing this," Eli told his friend.

Theodore grinned. "Eli, I thought I'd never see the day."

"I've been waiting most of my life for *that* girl," Eli admitted, looking at Jules.

"Well, if you don't have any objections, let's get started. The wife and I have dinner plans at seven."

"Oh, yeah, we'll have you out of here in plenty of time." Eli smiled and reached his hand out for Jules's. Theodore asked the two women who owned the inn to be the witnesses, and they readily agreed.

"This is a wonderful day for the two of you," he began, "and I'm honored Eli asked me to be part of it. I've known him for a good little while now, and I often wondered if this day would come for Eli—not because he didn't know what love was, but because he always seemed to be looking for it and not finding it. Now I know why he didn't find it at Brown: Jules wasn't there. She was off becoming the woman who was going to marry Eli."

With tears in his eyes, Eli smiled at Jules as he held her hands in his.

"Eli, do have your vows prepared?" Theodore asked, and Eli nodded.

"Jules, you're the most incredible woman I've ever known," Eli said, "and I've been in love with you since I was fifteen. Six months ago, when I saw you sitting in your dad's office, I knew I was going to marry you. I can't believe I'm getting my chance after all these years. Jules, you already have my heart, so it makes perfect sense that I'll love you in this life, the next, and the one after that. My powers of prediction don't show me the future, but I know that no matter what happens…if we're together, we can handle it. I love you today, tomorrow, and forever…even when you're mad at me or I'm mad at you. I promise to always be faithful and to communicate." A few tears fell down his face as he pushed the wedding band and engagement ring on to her finger.

Jules was doing her absolute best not to lose it. "Eli, I love you," she said, her lips quivering, "and ever since you proposed to me, a constant thought has been in my head." Eli took a deep breath and looked pensive. "It's a line from *Top Gun*." She smiled, and he chuckled. "There are hearts breaking wide open all over the world tonight because Eli King is off the market."

That made Eli laugh. "And I'm one hundred percent, prime time in love with you," he finished the line for her.

"You're the most beautiful man, inside and out, and your knowing the rest of that line shows how well you know me. That's what it all comes down to, isn't it? Finding your person. The person who loves you no matter what. Eli, I'm your person, and you're mine. You have my heart too. I love you today, tomorrow, and forever…even when you're mad at me or I'm mad at you. I promise to always be faithful and to communicate." She repeated his words with shaky lips and more than a few tears breaching the surface while she pushed his wedding band over the knuckles on his ring finger. He gently grabbed her face and kissed her. The women who owned the inn were dabbing their eyes and wiping their noses as they smiled.

"You beat me to it," Theodore said with a grin, "so I now pronounce you husband and wife."

Eli and Jules smiled at each other as their lips met again. After the ceremony, everyone put their signatures on all the necessary paperwork. Eli and Jules thanked Theodore again for coming then said good-bye and headed to the dining room for dinner: salad first, then lobster, filet mignon, garlic-parmesan mashed potatoes with brown gravy, and broccoli, cauliflower, and onions.

After eating as much as they could without being gluttonous, they both devoured a cupcake from the half dozen Jules had ordered for the occasion. Upstairs, in their room, they quickly shed their clothes and made love late into the night.

Sexually exhausted, Jules passed out in his arms after she exhaled, "I love you, husband."

Eli lay on his back, with his wife wrapped in his arms, and took the first easy breath he'd taken since the moment she'd told him she'd been raped as a teenager. He knew they'd have to go back to Boston on Sunday—life had to continue, but now it could continue with their being married. Their union was now recognized by law; they belonged to each other.

❧ ❧

They arrived back at Eli's place late Sunday afternoon. He insisted on carrying Jules across the threshold as they walked in. He unlocked the door, picked her up, and carried her inside. The first thing they did was put their rings and marriage license in the safe in Eli's bedroom. Jules was going to have to go back to her parents' house soon because Mondays were busy days for Lovey. However, Eli wasn't going to spend the second night of his marriage away from his wife. So he packed a bag and went with Jules to her parents' house, where'd they spend the night in the family room, curled up on the sofa together.

Chapter 17

April, two weeks before the trip to Jamaica

*L*ife seemed easier, and Eli definitely seemed calmer. For months the two of them had tried not to look like they were keeping a secret. Lovey was having lunch with Martha at the Langham, and Jules had called Eli to see if he wanted to join her for lunch at there as well. Of course he obliged. They were sharing an appetizer of crispy pork belly with roasted Brussels sprouts when his phone buzzed.

He looked up at her. "Two minutes, baby." He got up and walked away from the table. When he was out of earshot, he answered his phone. It was Mickey O'Malley.

"Eli, can you come by the bar sometime today?"

"I'm having lunch with my—with Jules. I'm having lunch with Jules right now, but can I come by after? Does two o'clock work for you?"

"I'll be here. Come upstairs," Mickey said.

Eli went back to lunch. Jules saved him a bite of that delicious pork belly. They shared their entrees and split a dessert. Lovey told Martha good-bye because she had an afternoon appointment, and then she was going to take nap. Eli walked them to the car. His kiss on Jules's lips made her stomach flutter.

"I'll see you tonight." Their lips touched again. "Your house or mine?" he asked.

"Yours, because when you kiss me, there's a spot between my legs that starts throbbing," she whispered into his ear.

"You're killing me, Mrs. King," he murmured as he hugged her. "I love you, babe." He kissed her lips again lightly.

"I love you back." She returned his kiss then got in the car to take Lovey to her appointment.

"He's already calling you 'Mrs. King'?"

"You heard that?"

Lovey nodded. "I also know you'll be staying at his house tonight."

Jules face burned scarlet as Lovey raised her eyebrows suggestively.

"Oh, honey, there's no need to be embarrassed. I'm so happy for you I almost can't stand myself."

∽∾ ∽∾

Eli went straight to O'Malley's. He did just as Mickey said and went upstairs when he arrived. Eli knocked on his office door, and Mickey called him inside. Mickey was seated at his desk, and Eli sat down across from him.

"I need to know how much you want to be involved in this, if at all."

"What conclusion did you come to, if I may ask?"

"Well, I'm not going to kill him, if that's what you're asking…but I can see why you want to. We can definitely make sure that his actions come back to him. Do you want to be involved?"

"I think he shouldn't be able to have kids, since Jules can't," Eli said, trying to control his anger.

"That's already included, along with all the other injuries she sustained. So again, do you want to be involved?"

"Yes, just tell me when and where," Eli replied.

"Aren't you getting married sometime soon?"

Eli nodded. "We're leaving for Jamaica in two weeks."

"When do you get on the plane?" Mickey asked.

"The Friday after next."

"Then it'll happen the Thursday night before you leave. You just have to get him over here," Mickey said matter-of-factly.

Eli nodded. "I can do that. One more thing…Jules's older brother, my best friend, Chris, has to be part of this too."

"Explain," Mickey snapped.

"The whole thing happened at a party Chris threw. They both convinced their mom that Jules would be okay because it was *his* party at *his* frat house. He called me a few months ago, right before I came to meet you actually. He wanted to tell me what happened to her, in case I didn't know. He was blaming himself and beating himself up. He just sounded like he still has a lot of guilt about it, you know? So I told him it wasn't his fault and asked him, if by chance, he remembered Denny Griffin being there."

"All right. He can be there but nobody else," Mickey snapped again.

"Nobody else knows. The only reason Chris knows is because he called me; otherwise I wouldn't have talked to him about what happened to Jules. We don't even say his name," Eli offered.

"Good. Keep it that way. People get caught 'cause they talk, but I don't have to tell you that. You're a lawyer." Mickey didn't snap this time.

Eli nodded.

"Come see me the Wednesday before unless you hear from me," Mickey directed.

"Yes, sir." Eli nodded again.

"Now get out of here," Mickey said with a grin.

⁓⁓⁓

Back at his office, Eli called Chris and told him that he'd be ready for his "big brother" speech the Thursday night before they left for Jamaica and that Chris had to make the one-hour drive from his home in Nashua, New Hampshire, to Boston to do it. He said they also had some important business to attend to, and Chris understood what he meant. After he ended their phone call, he went back to work. He was trying to do everything necessary to keep his mind busy. Eli planned to work until Jules would be off "Lovey duty" and free to go home with him.

⁓⁓⁓

The next week and a half left Eli feeling anxious. He dealt with it by going to the gym every day. Mickey hadn't given him any details about what would happen Thursday night, and Eli was trying to keep his overactive brain from going into overdrive and overheating, because that was about where he was right now. Early Monday afternoon, after he changed into his work clothes and left the gym, he went into one of his favorite delis, McAlister's, in search of food. A twist of fate put him there at right time, because Denny Griffin was two people ahead of him in line. Eli played it cool and aloof, as if he hadn't seen him. Denny was waiting for his order when he spotted Eli.

"Hey, Eli. How's it going?" Denny started.

"Hey, man. Good. And you?" Eli was short.

"I'm working my ass off right now."

"I know how that goes…but listen, if you're not busy Thursday night, some people are getting together at O'Malley's to watch Boston and Baltimore," Eli informed him. He watched Denny hesitate, as if he were going to decline the offer. "Jules probably will be there too." Eli felt sick saying it, but those were the magic words.

As Denny's eyes widened slightly, and his eyebrows rose a little, Eli knew he had him.

"What time?" Denny asked.

"Eight o'clock."

"Eight o'clock at O'Malley's on Thursday night," Denny repeated.

"Yeah, man. See you there; don't forget," Eli said, as he grabbed his to-go bag and headed out of the deli.

Eli went straight to work, closed the door to his office, and sat down in his chair. He put his head in his hands and rubbed his face. Hate was a new feeling for Eli; it made his guts hurt. Suddenly his cell buzzed. It was Mickey.

"Hello," Eli said.

"Hey, kid, what time you coming by Wednesday?"

"I'm done at five. Does that work for you?"

"You know where I'll be," Mickey said before hanging up.

The churning of the muscles in Eli's stomach made him feel as if he would explode. He wasn't sure he would be able to get anything done at the office. To his surprise, it occurred to him that he needed to calm down, and he also needed to eat. He grabbed his to-go bag, his laptop, and his keys, then headed for his car. He went home and found Jules's bowl and her green. Ten minutes later his head was numb, and he was hungry. After he finished his pastrami sandwich and chips, he found his laptop and grabbed the bowl again. After that, Eli had an incredibly productive two hours. Most of what he needed to get done got done.

⟡⟡⟡

On Wednesday night, Mickey was in his office, meeting with Eli. "Do you know if he's coming tomorrow night?" he asked.

"Yeah, I saw him on Monday and told him some guys were getting together to watch the game. He hesitated, so I told him Jules would be here."

"How you doing with that?" Mickey asked.

Eli frowned. "I was sick all day from telling him that, but he's coming. I saw it all over his face."

"He's obsessive and narcissistic. With the mention of her name, of course he's coming. Listen, I have a couple of guys that do the heavy stuff. You can't get married with bruised and battered knuckles."

"No, I'd definitely have some explaining to do," Eli quipped.

"All right, this is set. Be here tomorrow night around seven thirty, and bring Jules's brother straight to my office when you get here."

"Okay, see you tomorrow night. And thanks again," Eli replied.

"Hey," Mickey said before Eli got up, "there's no stopping this once it's in motion."

Eli shrugged. "That thought never crossed my mind. I just want him to experience even half the damage he did to her."

"That I can guarantee. Now get outta here. See you tomorrow at seven thirty."

Surprisingly, Wednesday night and Thursday day passed quickly. Jules was floating around like she'd mixed a few different strains of bud, and since she was already married to the man of her dreams, she truly was floating.

Eli didn't go home after work on Thursday; he knew it would be infinitely harder to leave if he saw her. Chris received a text to come to the law office instead of going to Eli's place. Philip left at five and locked the door behind him. Thomas Dempsey had spent the day tying up loose ends before the long weekend. Everyone was getting on a plane Friday morning and heading for Runaway Bay, Jamaica. All the guests would arrive Friday, relax Saturday, and attend the ceremony on Sunday.

When Chris showed up at his father's law office around six thirty, the doors were locked. Eli was sitting at his desk when his phone rang. When he answered, Chris said, "Come open the door."

Eli unlocked the door and embraced his best friend. They made their way back to his office and each took a seat in the comfortable chairs facing the windows that overlooked the city.

Chris looked similar to Aaron. They were both more than six feet tall, but Chris was an inch or two taller than his brother. They both had dark-auburn hair and darker eyes. Thomas Dempsey's sons favored him much more than his daughter ever did.

Eli spoke first. "You know I didn't ask you to come to Boston to give me your 'big brother' speech, right? I'm more than willing to listen to you, but let's do that in Jamaica, after we get done with tonight. Tonight has been a long time coming."

"What's going on, Eli?" Chris wondered.

"Mickey O'Malley has arranged to help us beat the shit out of Denny Griffin," Eli confided.

"You're kidding." Chris sounded impressed.

Eli shook his head. "They're not going to kill him, but he's probably going to need physical therapy when we're done. Just remember that we can't hit him too many times with our fists. We can't show up to my wedding with busted knuckles."

"Agreed," Chris replied.

"When Denny gets to O'Malley's, let him order a drink, and then we'll make our way upstairs. I don't plan on being there long. And you have to get back home to Nashua so you and your family can catch a plane tomorrow."

"You think we should head over there now?" Chris asked.

"Yeah, I want to get there before Denny does," Eli said, grabbing his keys and phone.

Chris and Eli drove over to O'Malley's then went straight upstairs to Mickey's office. Mickey was on the phone when they walked in and sat down. Chris was doing his best to hold his angst at bay; he hadn't seen Denny in years. Although he'd heard of Mickey O'Malley, he didn't know him personally, and he'd never been in a fight. He and Eli weren't brawlers—they used their brains not their fists.

"This her brother?" Mickey asked.

"Yes, this is Chris Dempsey," Eli said, as Chris extended his hand to meet Mickey's.

"Listen, you two aren't doing most of this ass kicking. I'll allow you a few hits each, but then you both have to go."

"What will you do then?" Chris asked.

"He'll get dropped off at the ER, and he'll get all patched up. It won't change the past—there still won't be any justice—but it'll feel good." Mickey cracked a smile.

"One problem." Chris spoke up, and Mickey glared at him. "I've never actually hit anybody before."

"That's okay. I wasn't planning on either of you using your hands anyway. Can you swing a bat?"

"I can," Chris affirmed.

"Then no need to worry. And I know I don't have to warn either of you that this never happened," Mickey said to a nodding Chris and Eli.

"You have the police report and the photos up here?" Eli asked.

Mickey nodded.

"Do me a favor and spread them out on the table," Eli requested.

"Okay, now you two get back downstairs. These guys have a few questions for me," Mickey snapped as he nodded toward his guys: Lloyd, David, and Boris.

Eli and Chris headed downstairs and found seats at the bar. They ordered a couple of beers, acclimated to their surroundings, and waited. Denny was already there. He was standing at the bar, talking to a couple of people. Eli spotted Mickey out the corner of his eye as he walked behind the bar.

"Everything's ready when you are," Mickey said, leaning over the bar. Eli looked at Chris, who finished his beer.

"Go ahead upstairs," he told Chris. "If he sees you, he might know something's up."

Chris didn't respond; he just got up and walked toward the back of the bar to go upstairs. Waiting in Mickey's office were three very large men who couldn't be seen from the top of the stairs.

In the other office, which adjoined Mickey's office, a long table was flush against the wall. Several items were spread out on top of it, including photographs, a few legal documents, some medical information, and a police report. Chris walked into the room and looked at some of the items. Lloyd, the muscle-clad "enforcer," walked up beside him and studied some of the photos.

"That's a fucked-up thing to do to someone," Lloyd spat.

"Yeah, this is my sister," Chris snarled, pointing to a photograph of Jules. "This guy, Denny, was supposed to be my friend, and he raped my sister."

"Oh, you're the brother. C'mon. Let's go into Mickey's office and wait." Chris did as instructed, following Lloyd, who closed the door to Mickey's office behind them.

Downstairs at the bar, Eli got off his stool and made his way over to Denny. There was a small crowd of people around him and a woman practically hanging off him. Eli hoped he didn't have to peel her off Denny to get him upstairs.

"Hey, man. Glad you made it," Eli said, faking enthusiasm.

"The more I thought about it, the more I realized I needed a little break," Denny replied.

"A gathering of locals is a good excuse to take a break from work." Eli sipped his drink.

"Alcohol and ass are definite stress relievers too. Is Jules here?" Denny said, before he tipped his Scotch up and finished it.

"I haven't seen her yet, but it's still early. Before you get completely out of work mode, I need your help with something," Eli baited him.

"Name it," Denny replied eagerly.

"The stuff is upstairs in one of the offices. I have a criminal case I'm working on that needs a fresh pair of eyes," Eli said, walking toward the stairs while Denny followed.

When they reached the top of the stairs, Eli led Denny into the empty office. Denny walked over to the table where the documents were spread out.

"Is this what you're working on?" he asked, holding up something from the table.

Eli nodded. He was waiting for Denny to look at what was in his hands. Denny looked down, and Eli *knew* that Denny *knew* what he was looking at.

"What is this?" Denny asked nonchalantly.

"Just look at it, and tell me what you think," Eli directed.

"Are you defending the accused?" Denny inquired.

"No, the victim," Eli said, and took a deep breath. While Denny was looking at the police report, Mickey came up the stairs, quietly entered the office, then closed the door behind him and locked it.

"To me, it looks like there's insufficient evidence to accuse anybody," Denny said nonchalantly.

Eli flicked his eyes to Mickey, who nodded once.

"I guess you would know, huh, Denny?" Eli stared at him.

"What the hell does that mean?"

"You know exactly what that means," Chris said, as he walked out of Mickey's office, baseball bat in hand, followed by three giant men.

"Chris Dempsey! What the fuck is going on?" Denny's eyes shifted to each man in the room.

"Denny, we need your help with something," Eli interjected.

"I don't know what this is about or what Jules told you—" Denny started.

"Nobody said anything about Jules," Eli interrupted. "But since you brought her up, let's talk about that."

"I'm not talking about anything. I'm outta here." Denny stepped forward to leave.

"Not so fast," Mickey snapped. "You've admitted to being in the same place at the same time this girl was hurt."

Denny acted confused. "What girl? Who was hurt?"

"You told Eli that you took her virginity at a party," Mickey snapped.

Denny stiffened for a moment. "So this *is* about Jules," he said with a smug look.

Everyone was quiet.

"What's wrong, Eli? You mad because I beat you to her?"

Denny barely got the words out of his mouth before Eli punched him in the stomach. He dropped to his knees. A steady stream of coughs and curses followed, and then Denny rose slowly back to his feet.

"Nah, Denny, I'm mad because you raped her, beat her, and left her for dead," Eli said, as he landed a solid punch to Denny's left kidney, which made his knees buckle. Denny let out a strangled breath as he used the table to stand again.

"Fuck, stop doing that!" Denny shouted.

"My sister wasn't able to say that since you gave her enough horse tranquilizer to kill her," Chris said, grabbing Denny by the collar.

"Look, man, I don't know what Jules told you guys…" Denny tried to explain.

"Answer me this," Mickey barked. "Did you take her out on a date the summer she started her senior year of high school? Before you answer me, I want you to think real hard and make sure you answer truthfully"—Mickey glared at him—"because if you lie, I'm going have these three guys go to town on you like a piñata. Now did you take her out on a date that you asked her mother's permission for?"

Denny nodded once; Chris still had him yanked up by his collar.

"Did you take her home at the end of the date that night?" Mickey asked.

Denny nodded again. Eli's eyes met Mickey's, and he shook his head slightly.

"David," Mickey commanded, and David delivered a blow to the same kidney Eli had pounded a minute ago. Chris continued to grip Denny's collar.

Denny yelped.

"Denny, Denny, Denny. I told you how important it was for you to tell the truth. See, David here is a boxer, and you're simply a punching bag. So I'm going to need you to do better, for your own sake. Make no mistake—you're going to get your shit pushed in, but right now you're making it harder on yourself. Now did you drop her off?"

"I don't know…I don't remember," Denny wailed. Mickey looked at David, who delivered a gut shot.

"Oh, Denny, not only do I think you remember, I think you relish the memories of chasing her and taking what you wanted. That night was the first time you tried to take advantage of this girl, who was several years younger than you. But you scared her, and she got away from you, and you left her in the middle of nowhere."

"I went back, but I couldn't find her," Denny admitted.

"Then, that winter, you found her in the basement of the school library," Mickey continued.

"I didn't do anything to her in the library," Denny snapped.

"You didn't have a chance to because the director interrupted you." Mickey nodded at David again. Before he could act, Chris dropped his collar, pushed Denny back an arm's length, picked up the bat, and swung it so it landed across his rib cage. Denny dropped to the floor.

"You were supposed to be my friend, *our* friend." Chris gestured toward Eli. "You were supposed to be my friend, and you raped my sister you piece of shit," he screamed, before he kicked Denny in the torso a couple of times. It was Lloyd who pulled Denny back up to a standing position.

"And since you didn't get what you wanted that time either," Mickey said, "you went to a party at her brother's frat house, and serendipitously, she was there."

Denny nodded, and so did Mickey. Lloyd held him while David landed another kidney shot. This time Denny exhaled a spittle of blood.

"Denny," Mickey said, "we don't need for you to admit that you're the one who drugged Jules, raped her, beat her, then left her to die. We just need for you to know that we know. Now we're not going to kill you, Denny, but you might wish you were dead when we're done. However, should you think of any type of retaliation for this, we'll just kill you and make it look like a carjacking. So you have to weigh the pros and cons: you can keep your mouth shut and realize that this is karma, or you can start talking nonsense and wind up in the morgue."

Mickey's quiet voice was laced with rage.

Denny began to protest, and it was bordering on begging. Then he asked, "What happens when karma finds *you?*"

"That bitch will shake my hand and thank me for the help," Mickey said matter-of-factly. "We're the good guys here, Denny. None of us drugged a teenage girl, then raped and beat her, nearly killing her in the process. You did that, and we're… correcting an imbalance, if you will. This should be a lesson for you to never repeat these behaviors, and if you already have, you'd better pray to your God that we don't find out about it."

"You scared, Denny?" Eli asked mockingly. "Good, 'cause I did this to you. Now shut up, you fucking pussy," he barked before he kicked him in the nuts and his elbow made contact with Denny's jaw. Lloyd picked up Denny's shaking body from the floor again.

"She never loved you—in fact she barely liked you," Eli spat out. "You may have been her first, not because you deserved to be, but because you took it, you stole it; she didn't give it to you."

Eli grabbed Denny by the face and got real close. "Denny, you have no idea how badly I want to kill you, but I won't. You also have no idea how close you came to having a former inmate's dick shoved repeatedly in your ass, because it's what you deserve, but we decided against that. These three fine men here are going to make sure you remember this because, unlike Jules, you won't have a dose of ketamine before ulti-mate destruction is brought upon your body."

Denny began to object, but Eli wasn't finished. He punched Denny in the stomach again.

"Shut. Up," Eli said, looking directly at him. "You don't get to talk. You don't get to talk to me. Furthermore, you don't ever get to speak to Jules again, ever. While I'm at it, keep your ass in Boston, because we won't be here. You can keep your cushy little life here, but since you took away Jules's ability to have children, don't count on ever having any yourself. And when you get mad about this, I want you to remember how lucky you are to still be alive with your rectal integrity intact."

The words had barely left Eli's mouth, and Mickey nod-ded toward the door for Eli and Chris to leave. That meant David, Lloyd, and Boris were going to go to work on Denny. Eli got Chris's attention, and they crossed the room to the door. Before they left, Mickey stopped them.

"You did good tonight, kid," he told Eli, "and don't worry—I've taken care of everything. The detective who will be 'investigating' this 'mugging' is my nephew. This was your wedding present from me and mine. Now get outta here and go get married." Mickey smiled as he patted Eli on the back.

"Thank you, sir. I'm forever grateful," Eli said, returning the smile.

"Yes, thank you," Chris added. "From the bottom of my heart, thank you. And if I had to meet *the* Mickey O'Malley, I'm glad it was this way, and not like Denny."

Mickey laughed. "I know you'll keep it that way." He nodded, and Eli and Chris headed downstairs.

As the front door to O'Malley's closed, Chris wrapped Eli in a "man hug." Ten years of guilt and repressed, undirected anger had dissipated; Chris no longer carried the burden that the trauma Jules had suffered was his fault.

"Get your ass home, showered, and in bed so you'll have the patience tomorrow to get your crew on a plane and then to us in Runaway Bay," Eli ordered, as if he were directing a movie. "Besides, I'm looking forward to that 'big brother' speech tomorrow over mojitos." Eli grinned and Chris chuckled.

"Okay, family, see you tomorrow in Jamaica," Chris said, before he got into his car and headed home to New Hampshire.

$\mathcal{J}$ules awoke the next morning to the sound of Eli's alarm sounding lightly. His lips covered hers before her eyes had even opened fully. At 5:00 a.m., they arrived at Logan Airport in a cab. They were standing curbside, checking their bags, when Talia, Eli's oldest sister, pulled up where the cab had been. She had chauffeured both sets of parents and Lovey to meet the bride and groom at the airport. Talia's and Sasha's families would be on the two o'clock flight. Aaron's and Chris's families would leave from the airport in Manchester, New Hampshire, around noon. This morning's flight would begin boarding at 6:10. By seven that evening, they'd all be together at the Sunset Villas in Runaway Bay, Jamaica.

Somewhere around that same time, a doctor at Mass General determined it necessary to put Denny Griffin in a medically induced coma due to the trauma his body had sustained. They would wake him up in about a week or so. Then the good doctors would determine how much physical therapy he would need.

It turned out that the detective didn't have much to go on in the way of Denny's case. Denny had been found in an alley, looking like he'd experienced his worst day on earth, with nothing but his clothing and his ID.

Eli still hadn't made up his mind whether he was going to tell Jules about the happenings of the previous night. Either way, he wasn't going to tell her this week. Denny was the last person either of them would be worried about for the next ten days. Truth be told, Eli was actually looking forward to the "big brother" speech Chris was going to give him. He was absolutely ecstatic about getting out of Boston, and he couldn't be happier to be celebrating his union with Jules in front of the people they loved most.

They landed at the airport in Kingston a little after noon. Thomas, Helene, and Lovey, along with Sam and Debra, decided to stay in Kingston until the rest of their families arrived. Both sets of parents were grandparents—the Dempseys had three, and the Kings had five—and they anticipated their grown children's need for assistance with the grandchildren. Helene suggested they find a restaurant and have a long, leisurely lunch. Jules and Eli were headed to the villas with their luggage in tow.

As the cab pulled up to the secluded villas, Jules asked, "What time is it?"

"Quarter to two." Eli looked at her. "You thinking what I'm thinking?"

She cocked an eyebrow at him, and a few moments later, she felt as though the driver couldn't unload the cab fast enough. It took nearly fifteen minutes before all the luggage was unloaded and put in the appropriate villa. This would be their last opportunity for uncensored sex until after their families left. Each couple/family had their own villa, but the villas were situated very close together. Eli and Jules could still get some lovin' in while their families were there; it'd just have to be more like "stealth sex"—quick and quiet. The luxurious villas were certainly extravagant, but Jules didn't think they were soundproof.

Eli kissed Jules feverishly as they made their way to the bed inside their villa. He sat down on the bed and reached up under her dress. Jules was only wearing a thong underneath it. He gripped the thin strings and slid the thong down her legs, and she stepped out of it.

"Mrs. King, I'm so in love with you," he said before her lips came crashing down on his while she climbed on top of his lap. Jules lightly gripped his face as her tongue tangled with his and his hands caressed her round bottom. She sat up and unbuttoned his pants, and then he leaned forward and lifted his shirt over his head. Then he flipped her over on her back and pulled her dress up around her waist.

"Want me to take it off?" Jules asked breathlessly.

"No, baby, I want to make love to you while you're wearing this dress so all night I can look at you and know that I made love to you while you were wearing it," Eli said, as he was kissing down her stomach. She caught his face in her hand and pulled his lips toward her face. Eli licked his fingers and touched the warmth between her legs.

He dropped his head and pressed his lips to hers. This was exactly the release he needed after the activities of the previous night. There were things he'd done for her that he'd never contemplated doing for anyone else: purchased clothes, proposed, committed assault and battery and probably conspiracy too. All she knew was that he loved her, and he wanted her to feel all the love he had for her.

Jules felt the silky, soft head of his rock-hard shaft as he pushed in slightly and stretched her. Then he pulled back some and pushed in farther. The friction against her clit was perfect. Those strong hips tilted up, changing the angle, and his nimble fingers found her aching bud. His strokes in and out were agonizingly slow, but they felt so damn good. He pushed her legs back, propped her hips up, and she came.

"Eee-lllii!" Jules screamed.

"Oh, baby, I love it when you scream my name," he growled into to the crook of her neck, and she bit down on his earlobe. "Shit, don't do that...I'm close," he said in a husky voice.

He stuck his tongue in her mouth, and she willingly accepted it by sucking on it. Just when she thought she couldn't take any more, he lightly pinched her clit between his finger and his thumb and used every finger to massage and stimulate it. Between that move and the enormous cock filling her, she came again.

"Yeah, baby...so good," she panted, and ran her nails down his back. He was grinding his hips into her pussy when he came, flooding her with warmth.

"Oh, Eli!" she exclaimed.

His toned, strong arms wrapped around her. Her legs were still wrapped around his waist as he relaxed into their embrace.

"Am I hurting you?" he asked.

"No, but this is my least favorite part," she confided.

"I love holding you, Jules," he admitted.

"I love it when you hold me too."

Eli looked confused. "Then what's your least favorite part?"

"When you pull out," she answered, and he chuckled with relief.

He kissed her on the forehead. "I love you, baby."

"I know, and I love you back." She smiled. "I guess we should shower. We smell like sweaty sex. And I know how you feel about shower sex, so I think we'll be safe showering together...you know, to conserve water and all."

"Shit, baby, after the shower, I'll be ready for round two," he said with a grin.

"Easy there, King Kong. I figure everyone will be here sooner rather than later, and I don't want to get busted, thank you."

Eli frowned. "Buzz kill."

She smiled at him. "You'll live, and you know I'm right."

"Yeah, yeah. I know," he conceded.

Over the next hour, they showered and unpacked, since they would be there for the next ten days. Jules put on the same dress that she was wearing when they arrived. When she walked into the kitchen area, Eli was making a large pitcher of mojitos. He was standing there looking amazing in a dark-blue linen shirt and camel-colored linen shorts.

Eli whistled. "I love that dress. Where have I seen it?"

Jules grinned. "If you like this one, you should see the one I'm wearing to the reception." Their eyes met, and he smiled back.

"Hey. My dad called about ten minutes ago. Everybody's in Jamaica safely, with all their luggage."

"Wow. That's a small miracle. How far away are they?"

"They should be here any minute," he replied.

"Let's go out and wait for them," Jules offered.

"You want a mojito while we wait?"

"No, I'm good, but enjoy your concoction, babe."

"Will you at least taste it?"

"Sure," she said, taking a sip of the delicious drink. "Maybe I'll have one once everyone is here," she thought aloud, as they headed out to meet their families.

It was nearly four o'clock when twenty-five people arrived in multiple taxis. Sam and Debra King were with their five grandchildren and their two daughters and sons-in-law. Thomas and Helene Dempsey were with their three grand-children, two sons, their daughters-in-law, and Lovey. Leslie and Jackie would come from Miami with Annette on Saturday afternoon. All these people were going to enjoy some relaxing time together and witness Eli and Jules commit themselves to each other again.

Once everyone was settled, Chris decided he was going to give Eli his "big brother" speech. Mojitos in hand, they walked the hundred feet down the dock to the beach and sat down in the sand. Eli didn't see Chris grab the pitcher and bring it with them.

As the families were already well acquainted, their inter-actions were effortless. All the children were playing together, so naturally all the ladies were talking and watching the chil-dren play in the shallow water off the dock. Surprisingly, the men were entertaining the children too.

"There can never be too many eyes on children," Sam said to Thomas as they set the boundary for the children in the water. Of course, since Thomas was a father and a grand-father too, he knew exactly the point Sam was making.

Back on the beach, Eli looked at Chris after he sipped his mojito, then said, "I'm ready for your 'big brother' speech… if you're so inclined."

"Eli, we've been best friends since we were eight years old, and I had absolutely no idea you liked my sister," Chris said, shaking his head. "And you're right, I wouldn't have liked it if you had tried to hook up with her when we were younger. But now…well, now it doesn't bother me the slightest. It didn't bother me when you called me about it; it was just unexpected. I'm actually glad it's you who's marrying my sister and not some douche bag named Wainwright who says idiotic shit like 'bro' and 'YOLO,' and only plays golf to advance his career."

"Dude, who is this guy you hate so much?"

"Nobody in particular. Look, you like your sisters' husbands, right?"

Eli nodded. "I actually do. Garrett and Nate have been family for a long time."

"Since you were the baby and saw how well your sisters' relationships worked out, you didn't have to worry about the infinite number of douche bags who could potentially try to attach themselves to Talia and Sasha."

Eli shuddered at the thought.

"I never imagined it would be you, but I'm glad it is. The best part about this is I don't have to give you the *real* 'big brother' speech, and I—"

"Hold on," Eli interrupted. "I'm supposed to be getting *the* 'big brother' speech. What the hell, man?"

Chris laughed lightly. "I don't have to threaten to kill you, Eli. I know just by the way you attend to my sister that you love her. I don't have to tell you any of the things I would say to some guy I don't know. Like I said, you're not some douche bag named Wainwright; you're my blood brother."

"Since the summer before fifth grade." Eli nodded and raised his glass.

"After last night, I know you love her." They shared a look.

"More than my life," Eli said.

"That's more than enough for me," Chris said, his hazel eyes shining.

Aaron walked over to where they were sitting on the beach. "So this is where the mojitos went," he said, taking the pitcher from Chris. "What are you two talking about?"

"Elijah marrying our little sister."

"That's a fascinating subject," Aaron said as he took a swig from the pitcher.

Eli winced. "Don't start."

"Eli loves Jules, Eli loves Jules," the brothers sang in unison.

"I sure do. Jeez." They all cracked up.

"Thank God she's not marrying some chump," Aaron said. "I actually can look forward to seeing you at family functions. This whole shit could've been so much worse. Jules could have fallen for some random guy; I heard my wife use the term 'rando.' You ever heard such nonsense? Anyway, now I won't have to dread having to make small talk with some dude I couldn't care less about."

"Have you two already had this conversation?" Eli directed his question to Aaron. "Chris said almost those exact words just now."

"We agreed on the plane that this was the best possible outcome of all the things that could've happened."

The three friends sat on the sand, sipped their mojitos, and watched their dads play with the children in the shallow water as the sun was setting. The parents eventually gathered the kids and took them inside to get them into dry clothes before the two families had dinner together.

❦

The next day, Saturday, was filled with numerous tasks to prepare for Sunday's events, and the crew from Miami would be arriving too. Everyone ate breakfast together, and then the women went into town while the men stayed with the children. Debra and Helene went to pick up the flowers and pay the photographer. The cake and the wedding canopy would be delivered tomorrow. Jules, along with Lovey, Sadie, Morgan, Talia, and Sasha, went to get their nails done.

Jules asked Sadie to wear her hair long and curly—nothing fancy. This manicure and pedicure was as much primping as Jules was going to do. After all the ladies got their nails done, Debra and Helene met them to hand off the flowers. Jules, her sisters-in-law, and Lovey returned to the villas with all the flowers for the ceremony while Debra and Helene did some primping of their own.

After lunch, Lovey and the children took naps, and the adults took advantage of the quiet time. Eli met Jules in the bedroom in their villa as she rubbed herself down with sun block and put on her strapless bikini.

"Going somewhere, Mrs. King?"

"I'm taking a towel to the warm, sandy beach to lie in the sun. Want to come with me, Mr. King?"

"Absolutely," he said, as he took off his shirt. He was still in his swim shorts from earlier in the day when he had played with the children. "Will you rub some sun block on my back?"

"Why of course. We wouldn't want you to burn," she said sweetly.

While they were lying on the sand, Jules asked, "So did you get the 'big brother' speech from Chris yet?"

"We did that yesterday while we were drinking mojitos and everybody was watching the children play in the water."

"How'd it go?"

"It's kosher with both Chris and Aaron. They're glad you're not marrying some random guy. Chris was going to put a world of fear into some poor soul, but he said that wasn't necessary. He knows I love you."

"Well, since the Dempsey Neanderthals are good, I suppose we can continue with our plans to marry," Jules said, rolling her eyes.

"Your brothers love you, and let's just say they won't complain about coming to family events. It'll be just like old times but better."

"So much better because you're all mine." She leaned over and kissed him lightly.

"You know it, baby," Eli said, kissing her back.

∽∾

Leslie, Jackie, and Annette arrived about an hour after Debra and Helene had returned. After the grandmothers had come back from town, they had taken over with the children while the granddads made dinner: chicken perlo to accompany the shrimp, crab, and grilled fish. Lovey enjoyed spending time with her daughter and Jackie since she hadn't seen either of them in the year since Joe had passed.

After dinner, good nights were exchanged, and the villas were quiet. Jules showered, dried her hair, and rubbed her sun-kissed skin with coconut oil.

Eli stared at her the whole time. "You make it impossible for me not to want you," he said from across the room.

"Oh, no, don't look at me like that."

"What?" he asked with a wry smile.

"You're lucky we're not doing this the traditional Jewish way. If we did, we couldn't see each other for a whole week before the wedding. Now behave yourself," Jules said, crawling into bed.

"I know…You're right. Besides, you're already my wife," he reminded her as she laid her head on his chest.

∼∼∼

Around two on Sunday, Eli went to his parents' villa so Jules could get ready. Before he left, he lightly took her face in his hands. "I'll see you under the canopy at five, Mrs. King."

"I'll be the one in the dress walking toward you, Mr. King," she quipped.

By four o'clock that afternoon, Jules had just finished strategically placing rollers in her hair. Helene was wrapping the rest of Jules's hair around a curling iron then pinning it in place.

"I'm so happy for you and Eli. You two really do belong together," Helene said with tears in her eyes.

"Those are happy tears right, Ma?"

"Oui, ma petite bijou."

"Good, because this is a happy day," Jules said, trying not to cry. "I love you, Ma. Thank you for all of this, in case

I didn't say it along the way. You and Debra really outdid yourselves."

"You're welcome, my sweet girl. Don't forget to thank Debra too."

"I feel like I need to thank her for helping you plan this *and* for making Eli."

Mother and daughter giggled, and then Helene said, "That's not a bad idea, *ma petite*. Okay, all done. I'm going to finish getting ready myself while you do your makeup. Let me know if you need anything."

"Okay, I will. *Je t'aime, Maman.*"

"Je t'aime, fille."

Jules curled her eyelashes then applied a tinted moisturizer with sunscreen in it and lightly dusted her face with loose powder. She used a shimmery blush stick to give her cheeks a dewy look. Then she applied a neutral eye shadow with just a touch of glitter, which made her green eyes sparkle; she used black mascara to thicken her lashes before applying pink lip gloss to her full lips.

Before she took her hair down, she slipped into her wedding dress. It was an A-line dress that stopped right above her knees. The color was stone, not exactly white, and the material was organza with a lace overlay; it also had a sweetheart neckline and a beaded waistline. Jules had decided that since they'd be standing in the sand, she didn't want to wear a long dress.

Jules looked radiant. Her hair hung in long, relaxed curls down her back, and her bangs were swooped to the left, away from her eyes. Sadie had done as Jules had asked and was wearing her hair curly. Her dress was knee-length too, but it looked more like a sundress and was a deep blue. The wedding party had decided to go barefoot since it was so much easier to stand in the sand without shoes. They extended the same offer to their families.

At 4:55, Thomas Dempsey knocked on the door of his daughter's villa.

Sadie greeted him. "She's ready," she said.

He hugged his daughter-in-law then stepped forward, his eyes watering. "You ready, kid?" he asked, looking at Jules.

"The question is 'Are you ready, Daddy?'"

"As ready as I'll ever be, so don't push it." He clearly was trying to hold it together. "Okay, Sadie," he said, "I'll see you down there in a few minutes."

"Don't forget your flowers," Sadie reminded Jules as she walked out of the villa to meet Chris under the marriage canopy.

"I'm going to tell you like I told Eli when he asked my permission to marry you: few things would make me happier," Thomas said. "Your future husband, who's waiting for you right now, by the way, loves you deeply. As your father, I've always worried what kind of man eventually would take my little girl away. You've always been so smart; I knew you wouldn't settle for some bonehead. Honestly, I haven't worried since Eli made me aware of his intentions," he finished, smiling.

"I love you, Daddy." Jules's voice shook as she fanned her eyes, trying not ruin her makeup.

"I know, kid. I love you too." He took her hand and placed it in the crook of his arm.

As they stepped out of the villa, she saw Eli standing in the distance at the edge of the canopy. Rabbi Levin stood in the middle, while Chris stood off to Eli's side and Sadie stood on the opposite side. Eli was wearing khaki linen pants and a white linen short-sleeve shirt. Chris wore a dark-blue linen shirt, similar to the color of Sadie's dress, and khaki linen pants.

"Ladies and gentlemen, may I have your attention?" Rabbi Levin began.

In a Jewish ceremony, the rabbi doesn't really "marry" the couple; the rings are used to symbolize a couple's commitment to each other. The rabbi was there because he'd known Eli since he was born, and he also was there to chant the Seven Blessings in both Hebrew and English.

After the blessings came the vows. Eli looked at Jules as he put her ring on her finger and said, "With this ring, you are made holy to me, for I love you as my soul. You are now my wife."

Jules took his ring in her shaking fingers and replied, "With this ring, you are made holy to me, for I love you as my soul. You are now my husband."

Rabbi Levin smiled as he placed a champagne glass wrapped in a cloth napkin on the sand. As Eli forcefully stepped on the glass with his heel, everyone heard the sound of glass breaking, and then the rabbi said, "Mazel tov! Please kiss your wife."

Eli flicked his eyes toward Rabbi Levin then back to Jules. "Oh, yeah! I almost forgot!" He smiled, taking her face in his hands. Eli hadn't taken his eyes off Jules since he had seen her walking toward him on the beach. He kissed her sweetly while everyone cheered and clapped. Jules thought she heard a few whistles, but that might have just been the wind whipping around her ears, whistling her happiness.

The wedding photos came next. Various combinations of family members were photographed to preserve the day's memories. The photographer had been taken pictures for about fifteen minutes when Jules looked up at Eli with a wide grin. "What?" he asked.

"I want a few pictures on the dock, but I want to change first," she said, as she walked away from him. Sadie followed her into the villa to help her.

"This dress is perfect, Jules," Sadie said, as she zipped up the iridescent pink dress Jules had worn when she had married Eli the first time at the B&B in Springfield.

"Eli loves it," Jules said, smiling.

Sadie smiled back. "I can see why."

"Oh, Sadie, you're so sweet. You really are a great sister-in-law. Thanks so much for standing with me today." Jules hugged her.

"It meant a lot that you asked me."

Jules opened the door to the villa to see that pictures were still being taken. As Eli turned his head to the right and saw his wife, he couldn't contain the rush of emotions. She was standing on the dock, wearing the dress he had given her—the one she had married him in.

Their favorite picture from their wedding in Jamaica was the one taken on the dock near sunset: Eli was standing behind her, looking down at her slightly, as Jules stood in his arms, wearing the dress that held so many beautiful memories—and now they both looked forward to making a lifetime more.